English
Travel around
the world

旅遊英語
萬用手冊

英語學習不再是紙上談兵！

背誦單字的同時，
也能學習生活中最常用的短語對話，
讓英語學習更生活化！

國家圖書館出版品預行編目資料

旅遊英語萬用手冊 ／ 張瑜凌編著. -- 初版.
-- 新北市：雅典文化, 民106. 01印刷
面； 公分. -- (英語工具書；12)
ISBN 978-986-5753-77-1(平裝附光碟片)
1. 英語 2. 旅遊 3. 會話
805. 188 105023473

英語工具書系列 12

旅遊英語萬用手冊

編著／張瑜凌

內文排版／王國卿

封面設計／姚恩涵

法律顧問：方圓法律事務所／涂成樞律師

總經銷：永續圖書有限公司　　CVS代理／美璟文化有限公司
永續圖書線上購物網　　　TEL：（02）2723-9968
www.foreverbooks.com.tw　FAX：（02）2723-9668

出版日／2017年1月

雅典文化

出　22103　新北市汐止區大同路三段194號9樓之1
版　　　　TEL　（02）8647-3663
社　　　　FAX　（02）8647-3660

【序言】
出國旅遊的必備手冊

　　「如果下星期就要出國了，有辦法在最短的時間內就學好英語嗎？」

　　「如果選擇出國度假自由行，該如何面對人在國外時，可能發生的種種問題呢？」

　　「有沒有簡單又實用的英語，能解決我短期國外生活的溝通問題？」

　　英語不應該成為你裹足不前的阻力，以上的困惑，您都可以在「旅遊英語萬用手冊」內得到解決的辦法！所謂「臨陣磨鎗，不亮也光」，誰說一定要會說流利的英語才可以出國？本書教你只要利用最簡單的英語，就能安排一段快樂的國外度假旅程！

　　「旅遊英語萬用手冊」根據出國旅遊的情境，彙整了一系列最實用的旅遊英語主題，搭配情境式對話，模擬國外旅遊的應對，而每一個主題還附上「同義例句」和「相關例句」的實用例句，讓您在學習的同時，也能增加語言會話的深度與學習範圍。您更可以藉由本書所附的 MP3 學習光碟，一對一跟隨老師朗讀，加強對口語英文的記憶深度！

　　從現在開始，您也有機會完成國外旅遊自由行的夢想，讓「旅遊英語萬用手冊」陪您一起遨遊世界吧！

Chapter 3

住宿

Chapter 4

飲食

Chapter 5

交通・觀光

Chapter 6

購物

Chapter 7

和警察打交道

Chapter 8

尋求協助

Chapter 1

搭飛機

English Travel around the World

預約機位

I'd like to make a flight reservation.
我要預約機位。

A：Good morning. This is Continental Airlines.
　　早安。這是大陸航空。

B：I'd like to make a flight reservation.
　　我要預約機位。

同義例句--

例 I'd like to make a reservation for a flight to Buffalo tomorrow.
我要預訂明天到水牛城的航班。

例 I'd like to book flight 108 on February 25th.
我要訂二月廿五日的 108 班次。

例 I'd like to book the first flight to Buffalo for February 25th.
我想預訂二月廿五日到水牛城的最早航班。

例 I want to make a reservation from Taipei to Buffalo.
我要預訂從台北到水牛城的機票。

查詢航班日期

Do you fly to Buffalo on February 25th?

你們有二月廿五日到水牛城的班機嗎？

實用會話

A：Do you fly to Buffalo on February 25th?
你們有二月廿五日到水牛城的班機嗎？

B：Let me check. Wait a moment, please.
讓我查一查。讓我查一查。請稍等！

A：Thanks.
謝謝！

B：Sorry, sir, we don't have any flights on next Sunday.
先生，很抱歉，我們下星期天沒有任何的航班。

同義例句

例 Do you fly to Buffalo on next Sunday?
你們有下星期天到水牛城的班機嗎？

例 Do you fly from Taipei to Buffalo on February 25th?
你們有二月廿五日從台北飛到水牛城的班機嗎？

例 What's the next earliest flight for Buffalo?
下一班最早到水牛城的班機是哪一班？

例 Could you check the boarding time for me?
你能替我查班機時刻表嗎？

訂機票　MP3 002

I'd like to book a 10 am flight.

我要訂十點鐘的那一個班次。

實用會話 ------------------------------------

A：Do you have another flight before February 25th?
　　你們有在二月廿五日之前的其他航班嗎？

B：Yes, there's a flight at 7 am and one at 10 am on February 19th.
　　有的，在二月十九日早上七點鐘有一班，還有一班是十點鐘。

A：OK, I'd like to book a 10 am flight.
　　好，我要訂十點鐘的那一個班次。

B：OK, sir. May I have your name, please?
　　好的，先生。請問你的大名？

相關例句 ------------------------------------

例 I prefer a morning flight.
　　我偏好早上的班機。

訂兩人的機票

I'd like to book two seats.

我要訂兩張機票。

實用會話 ------------------------------------

A：This is Continental Airlines. May I help you?
　　這是大陸航空。需要我幫忙嗎？

B：I'd like to book two seats.
我要訂兩張機票。

A：Please give me both of your names.
請給我二位的名字。

B：It's Charlie Brown and Sandy Smith.
查理・布朗和珊蒂・史密斯。

(同)(義)(例)(句)--

例 I'd like to book two seats from Taipei to Buffalo on May
25th.
我要訂五月廿五日兩個人從台北到水牛城的機票。

例 Are there two seats available on the 4 pm flight?
下午四點鐘起飛的班機還有兩個空位嗎？

訂來回機票	

I'd like to book a round-trip ticket.

我要訂一張來回機票。

(實)(用)(會)(話)--

A：Good afternoon. This is Continental Airlines.
午安。這是大陸航空。

B：Hi, I'd like to book a round-trip ticket.
嗨！我要訂一張來回機票。

A：Where do you plan to go, sir?
先生，你計畫去哪裡？

B：From Taipei to New York.
從台北到紐約。

A：No problem, sir.

　　沒問題的，先生。

找不到符合時間的航班

I can't make it until the 25th of February.

我二月廿五日前無法成行。

 實用會話 --

A：We have a flight on February 25th.

　　我們二月廿五日有班機。

B：I see. But I can't make it until the 25th of February.

　　我了解，可是我二月廿五日前無法成行。

A：I'm sorry, sir, that's the only flight we have.

　　很抱歉，先生，那是我們僅有的一個班次。

同義例句 --

例 But I'm looking for a nonstop flight from New York to Buffalo.

　　但是我在找從紐約直飛水牛城的班機。

直達航班

 MP3 004

I'd like to book a nonstop flight to Paris.

我想預訂到巴黎的直達航班。

實用會話--

A：This is Continental Airlines. May I help you?
這是大陸航空。需要我幫忙嗎？

B：I'd like to book a nonstop flight to Paris.
我想預訂到巴黎的直達航班。

A：What time do you prefer?
你偏好什麼時間？

B：Between 10 am and 4 pm.
從早上十點到下午四點鐘。

相關例句--

例 I'd like to book a nonstop flight from Taipei to Paris.
我想預訂從台北到巴黎的直達航班。

例 I'd like a nonstop flight.
我要訂直達的班機。

轉機航班

I'd like a stopover flight.
我要訂轉機的班機。

實用會話 --

A：I'd like to book a seat to Paris.
　　我想預訂到巴黎的航班。

B：Where are you planning to depart?
　　你要從哪裡離境？

A：From New York. I'd like a stopover flight.
　　從紐約。我要訂需要轉機的班機。

同義例句 --

例 I'd like a stopover flight to Buffalo.
　　我要訂到水牛城的轉機班機。

相關例句 --

例 I prefer to stop over in Hong Kong.
　　我比較喜歡在香港轉機。

例 I'm thinking of flying from Paris to New York on
　　February 1st and from New York to Taipei on February
　　8th.
　　我打算二月一日從巴黎到紐約，然後二月八日從紐約到台北。

離境的時間

I'm planning to depart on February 25th.

我打算在二月廿五日離境。

A：When do you want to leave?
　　你想什麼時候離境？

B：I'm planning to depart on February 25th.
　　我打算在二月廿五日離境。

A：OK. We have a flight on this Wednesday.
　　好的！我們這個星期三有航班。

B：Wednesday? OK. I'll book this flight.
　　星期三？好，我要訂這一個航班。

同義例句 ---

例 I'll leave Taipei at noon.
　　我中午就會離開台北。

例 I'll depart tomorrow.
　　我明天就會離境。

例 I'm planning to depart tomorrow night.
　　我計畫明天晚上離境。

例 I'll leave for Seattle tomorrow.
　　我明天會動身去西雅圖。

不限定航班的時間

Please leave the return ticket open.

回程機票請不要限定班次時間。

實用會話 --------------------------------------

A：I'd like to book a round-trip ticket from Taipei to Buffalo.

我要訂一張台北到水牛城的來回機票。

B：When do you want to depart?

你想要什麼時候離境？

A：This Friday. By the way, please leave the return ticket open.

這個星期五。還有，回程機票請不要限定班次時間。

B：No problem, sir.

沒問題的，先生！

票價

How much is the airfare?

機票是多少錢？

實用會話 --------------------------------------

A：How much is the airfare?

機票是多少錢？

B：It's two thousand dollars.

兩千元。

同義例句 --

例 I'd like to know the airfare.
我想要知道票價。

例 What's the fare from Taipei to Buffalo?
從台北到水牛城的票價是多少錢？

相關例句 --

例 What's the one-way fare?
單程票價是多少錢？

例 What's the round-trip fare?
回程票價是多少錢？

取消／變更機位

I want to cancel my reservation.
我想取消我的訂位。

 實用會話 --

A：This is Continental Airlines. May I help you?
這是大陸航空。需要我幫忙嗎？

B：I'd like to cancel my reservation.
我想取消我的訂位。

A：OK, sir, may I have your name?
好的，先生，請問你的大名？

相關例句 --

例 I'd like to cancel a flight for Mr. Brown.
我想替布朗先生取消機位。

例 I'd like to change my flight.
我想變更我的班機。

 MP3 007

再確認機位

I'd like to reconfirm my flight.

我要再確認我的機位。

 實用會話 --

A：Continental Airlines. May I help you?
　　這是大陸航空。需要我幫忙嗎？

B：I'd like to reconfirm my flight.
　　我要再確認我的機位。

A：OK, sir. Your name, please.
　　好的，先生。你的大名？

B：My name is David Jones.
　　我是大衛‧瓊斯。

A：OK, sir. Wait a moment, please.
　　好的，先生。請稍等！

同義例句 --

例 I'd like to reconfirm a flight for Mr. Brown.
我想替布朗先生再確認機位。

相關例句 --

例 I'd like to confirm my connecting flight reservations, please.
我要確認我的轉機航班。

何處辦理登機報到

Where may I check in for my flight?

我可以在哪裡辦理登機手續？

實用會話 --

A：May I help you?
需要我幫忙嗎？

B：Yes. Where may I check in for my flight?
是的！我可以在哪裡辦理登機手續？

A：Let me see your ticket.
我看看你的機票。

B：Here you are.
在這裡。

A：OK. Go straight ahead, and turn right then you will see the counter of Continental Airlines.
好，直走，然後右轉，你就會看到大陸航空的櫃台。

B：I see. Thank you so much.
我知道了。非常感謝你。

同義例句 --

例 Where can I check in for CA Flight 102?
我可以在哪裡辦理 CA102 班機的登機手續？

是否可以辦理報到

Can I check in now?
我現在可以辦理登機手續嗎？

實用會話---

A：May I help you?
　　需要我幫忙嗎？

B：Can I check in now?
　　我現在可以辦理登機手續嗎？

A：OK, sir. Passport and visa, please.
　　好的，先生。(請給我) 護照和簽證。

B：Here you are.
　　在這裡。

同義例句---

例 Can I check in for CA Flight 102 now?
　　我現在可以辦理 CA102 班機的登機手續嗎？

相關例句---

例 What time should I have to be at the airport?
　　我應該什麼時候到機場報到？

辦理登機報到

Check-in, please.
我要辦理登機。

實用會話 --------------------------------------

A：May I help you?
需要我幫忙嗎？

B：Check-in, please.
我要辦理登機。

A：May I have your passport and flight ticket, please?
請給我你的護照和機票。

B：Here you are.
在這裡。

A：Here is your boarding pass. Your seat is 22C.
Please be at your boarding gate one hour before
the flight departs.
這是你的登機證。你的座位是 22C。請在飛機起飛前一個小時
登機。

同義例句 --------------------------------------

例 I'd like to check in.
我要辦理登機。

相關例句 --------------------------------------

例 Is this the right counter to check in for this flight?
這個航班是在這個櫃檯辦理登機手續嗎？

報到劃位　009

May I have a window seat?
我可以要靠窗戶的座位嗎？

實用會話 --

A：Check in, please.
　　我要辦理登機，謝謝！

B：Would you like a window or an aisle seat?
　　你要靠窗戶還是靠走道的座位？

A：May I have a window seat?
　　我可以要靠窗戶的座位嗎？

B：OK, sir. We have one near the front of the cabin
　　on the left side.
　　好的，先生。我們有一個座位靠近機艙前段的左側。

A：That should be fine.
　　太好了！

同義例句 --

例 I want an aisle seat.
　　我想要一個靠走道的座位。

例 I'd prefer a window seat.
　　我偏好靠窗戶的座位。

例 I don't want the aisle seat.
　　我不要靠走道的座位。

相關例句 --

例 Do you have any seating preference?
　　你有特別想坐在哪裡嗎？

要求特定區域的座位

Please give me a window seat.

請給我靠窗戶的座位。

實用會話 --

A：Passport and flight ticket, please.
請給我護照和機票。

B：Here you are.
在這裡。

A：Where would you like to sit?
你想坐在哪裡？

B：Please give me a window seat.
請給我靠窗戶的座位。

A：Sure, I'll do my best. Oh, there are no window seats left.
好的！我盡量！喔，沒有靠窗戶的座位了！

B：OK. An aisle seat then, but not a middle one, please.
好。那就靠走道的座位，但是不要在中間，謝謝！

相關例句 --

例 I'd like an emergency exit seat.
我想要靠緊急出口的座位。

例 I'd like a window seat near the front of the cabin.
我想要靠近前面機艙的座位。

詢問座位所在的區域

MP3 010

Is it an aisle seat?

這是靠走道的座位嗎？

實用會話 --

A：Is it an aisle seat?
　　這是靠走道的座位嗎？

B：No, it's not. It's a window seat.
　　不，這不是。這是靠窗的座位。

A：I'd like an aisle seat.
　　我想要靠走道的座位。

B：Let's see. OK, there is an aisle seat left.
　　我看看。好的，剛好有剩下一個靠走道的座位。

A：Thank you so much.
　　非常感謝！

相關例句 --

例 Is it a window seat?
　　這是靠窗戶的座位嗎？

例 Is it a middle seat?
　　這是在中間的座位嗎？

行李托運的數量

I have three pieces of baggage to check in.

我有三件行李要托運。

A：How many pieces of baggage do you have?
你有多少件行李？

B：I have three pieces of baggage to check in.
我有三件行李要托運。

A：Please put them on the scale.
請把它們放在秤上(過磅)。

B：Sure.
好的！

相關例句

例 I have these suitcases to check in.
這些是我要托運的行李。

例 How many suitcases can I take on a Continental Airlines flight?
搭乘大陸航空的班機我可以帶多少件行李箱？

被要求行李要辦理托運

You'll have to check in your bag.

你的袋子需要辦理托運。

A：How many pieces of hand baggage do you have?
你有幾件手提行李？

B：I'll keep this one as a carry-on.
這個是隨身的袋子。

A：Sir, your carry-on bag is too big and overweight.
先生，你隨身的袋子太大又超重。

B：I know, but...
我知道，但…

A：Sorry, sir, I'm afraid you'll have to check in your bag.
先生，很抱歉，你的袋子恐怕需要辦理托運。

相關例句 --

例 Any baggage to check in?
有行李要托運嗎？

例 How many pieces of baggage are you checking in?
你有多少件行李要托運？

攜帶隨身行李登機

I'll keep this bag as my hand baggage.

這個是我的隨身行李。

A：Do you have any baggage to check in?
你有任何行李要托運的嗎？

B：No. I'll keep this bag as my hand baggage.
沒有，這個是我的隨身行李。

同義例句 --

例 I just have this carry-on bag.
我只有這件隨身的袋子。

相關例句 --

例 How many carry-ons may I take on the plane?
我可以帶多少件隨身行李上飛機？

例 I have a suitcase and a carry-on bag.
我有這個行李和這個隨身袋子。

例 Can I carry this bag with me?
我可以隨身帶這個袋子嗎？

行李超重費用　

How much is the extra charge?
超重費是多少？

實用會話

A：Please put your luggage on the scale.
請你把的行李放在磅秤上（過磅）。

B：Is my luggage overweight?
我的行李有超重嗎？

A：I'm afraid so.
可能有喔！

B：How much is the extra charge?
超重費是多少？

A：Let's see. You have to pay $20 for excess baggage.
我看看！你要付二十元的行李超重費。

相關例句

例 What are your charges for excess baggage?
你們的行李超重費是多少？

例 It's at least 20 pounds overweight, isn't it?
它至少超重 20 磅，對吧？

通過金屬探測門

There are metal objects in your bag.

你的袋子裡有金屬物品。

實用會話 --

A：Please step through the security gate.
請通過安檢門。

B：Sure.
好！

A：Sir, do you have any metal items in your bag?
先生，你袋子裡有攜帶任何的金屬物品嗎？

B：I think I removed them all.
我覺得我已經全部取出了！

A：I am afraid I'm gonna have to check your bag.
我恐怕要檢查你的袋子。

B：OK.
好的！

A：There are metal objects in your bag. What is this?
你的袋子裡有金屬物品。這是什麼？

B：Oh, it's a pair of scissors.
喔，是一把剪刀！

A：I'm afraid that you can't take it onto an airplane.
I'll keep it, OK?
你恐怕不能攜帶這個上飛機，我會沒收，可以嗎？

繳交稅款

MP3 013

How much is the duty on this?

這個要付多少稅金呢？

A：You have to pay duty on the excess.
　　你要付超重費。

B：How much is the duty on this?
　　這個要付多少稅金呢？

同義例句 --

例 How much is the duty?
　　稅金是多少？

例 How much did you say?
　　你說是多少？

例 How should I pay for it?
　　我應該要如何付呢？

確認登機時間

What's the boarding time?

登機時間是什麼時候？

A：May I help you?
　　需要我幫忙嗎？

B：What's the boarding time?
登機時間是什麼時候？

A：At eight o'clock, forty minutes before departure.
八點鐘，是離境前的四十分鐘。

B：Thanks a lot.
多謝了！

同義例句 ---

例 What time can we start boarding?
我們什麼時候可以開始登機？

例 What time will boarding start?
什麼時候開始登機？

例 What time does boarding start?
什麼時候開始登機？

出境登機　

You need to be at the gate by ten am.
你要在早上十點鐘前抵達登機門。

實用會話 ---

A：May I help you?
需要我幫忙嗎？

B：What time will boarding start?
什麼時候開始登機？

A：Let me see your boarding pass.
給我看你的登機證。

B：Here you are.
在這裡。

A：Let's see. You need to be at the gate by ten am.
我看看，你要在早上十點鐘前抵達登機門。

(相)(關)(例)(句)--

例 Will the flight depart on time?
班機準時起飛嗎？

例 Is the plane on schedule?
飛機會準時嗎？

例 The flight arrived on schedule.
那班飛機準時抵達。

例 The flight is an hour behind schedule.
那班飛機誤點一個小時。

詢問何處登機

Where should I board?

我應該到哪裡登機？

(實)(用)(會)(話)--

A：Excuse me.
請問一下。

B：May I help you?
需要我幫忙嗎？

A：I'm on a Continental Airlines flight.
我要搭乘大陸航空公司班機。

B：Yes?
請説。

A：Where should I board?
我應該到哪裡登機？

B：Let me see your boarding pass.
給我看你的登機證。

相關例句--

例 What's the gate number?
登機門是幾號？

例 I don't know where I should board.
我不知道我應該在哪裡登機。

例 Where is the boarding gate?
登機門在哪裡？

例 Which way is Gate 2?
二號登機門是在哪個方向？

指示登機門的方向 015

You'll see it on your right side.
你就會看到在你的右手邊。

實用會話--

A：Where should I board?
我應該到哪裡登機？

B：It's Gate 2.
是二號登機門。

A：Can you direct me to Gate 2, please?
　　請問二號登機門怎麼走？

B：Go straight ahead, and you'll see it on your right side.
　　往前直走，你就會看到在你的右手邊。

A：Thanks a lot.
　　多謝啦！

相關例句--

例 Can you direct me to Gate 2, please?
　　請問二號登機門怎麼走？

走錯登機門

I am at the wrong gate.

我走錯登機門了。

實用會話--

A：May I help you?
　　需要我幫忙嗎？

B：It's time for me to board my plane, but...
　　我要登機了，但是…

A：Yes?
　　請說！

B：I think I am at the wrong gate.
　　我想我走錯登機門了。

A：What's your boarding gate number?
　　你的登機門是幾號？

B：It's Gate 5.
　　是五號登機門。

A：This way, please.
　　這邊請！

(相)(關)(例)(句)---

例 Which gate will I board at?
　　我要到哪個登機門？

例 Can you direct me to Gate 2, please?
　　可以告訴我二號登機門在哪裡嗎？

在機場內迷路

How should I get to terminal four?
四號航廈要怎麼走？

(實)(用)(會)(話)---

A：Excuse me.
　　請問一下！

B：Yes?
　　請說！

A：How should I get to terminal four?
　　四號航廈要怎麼走？

B：Let's see... go straight ahead until the post office
　　and turn right, you'll see the sign on your left side.
　　我看看…直走到郵局，然後右轉，你就會在你的左手邊看到標
　　誌。

A：Thank you.

　　謝謝！

準備登機

May I see your boarding pass?

可以給我看你的登機證嗎？

實用會話 --

A：We'd better board the plane now.

　　我們最好現在就登機。

B：OK, let's go.

　　好，我們走！

C：May I see your boarding pass?

　　可以給我看你的登機證嗎？

A：Here you are.

　　在這裡。

C：OK. Have a nice trip.

　　好了！祝你旅途愉快！

詢問轉機　　　　　　　　　　　　　　　　　　　 017

How to change planes for a connecting flight?

要如何轉搭轉機班機？

A：Excuse me.

　　你說什麼？

B：I'm in transit to New York.
我要轉機到紐約。

A：What can I do for you?
需要我幫什麼忙的嗎？

B：How to change planes for a connecting flight?
要如何轉搭轉機班機？

例 How should I transfer?
我要如何轉機？

例 How do I transfer to Buffalo?
我要如何轉機到水牛城？

尋找轉機櫃臺

How can I get to the connecting flight counter?

我要如何到轉機櫃臺？

A：How can I get to the connecting flight counter of Continental Airlines?
我要如何到大陸航空的轉機櫃臺？

B：It's over there, next to the post office.
就在那裡，在郵局的旁邊。

A：Thank you so much.
非常感謝你。

表明轉機身分　MP3 018

I'm a transit passenger.

我是轉機乘客。

實用會話 -

A : What can I do for you?
　　需要我幫什麼忙的嗎？

B : I'm a transit passenger. How should I transfer to Buffalo?
　　我是轉機乘客。我要如何轉機到水牛城？

A : OK. Let me see your transit card.
　　好的！給我看看你的轉機證。

B : Sure. Here you are.
　　好！在這裡。

A : Seven thirty p.m. Your boarding gate is 6.
　　晚上七點半，你的登機門是六號。

同義例句 -

例 I'm a transit passenger for Flight CA301.
　　我是搭乘 CA301 航班的轉機乘客。

例 I'm a transit passenger for this flight.
　　我是搭乘這個航班的轉機乘客。

辦理轉機

I'm connecting with AE709.

我要轉搭 AE709 班機。

 實用會話 --

A：Good morning, madam.
早安，女士。

B：Good morning. I'm connecting with AE709.
早安。我要轉搭 AE709 班機。

A：OK. May I have your transit card, please?
好的。請給我你的轉機證。

B：Here you are.
在這裡！

同義例句 --

例 I'm in transit.
我要轉機。

例 I'm in transit to Buffalo.
我要轉機到水牛城。

例 I'm continuing on to Buffalo.
我要繼續前往水牛城。

過境停留的時間

How long will we stop here?

我們會在這裡停留多久？

A：How long will we stop here?
　　我們會在這裡停留多久？

B：About 2 hours.
　　大約二個小時。

A：Thanks. Honey, it's still early now.Would you like something to drink?
　　謝謝！親愛的，現在還很早！你想喝點什麼嗎？

C：Yes, I want a cup of coffee.
　　好啊！我想喝一杯咖啡。

例 How long is the stopover?
　　過境要停留多久？

相關例句

例 When are we going to leave here?
　　我們什麼時候要離開這裡？

Chapter 2

登機出關

English Travel around the World

MP3 020

開始登機

Welcome aboard.

歡迎登機！

A : May I see your boarding pass, please?
　　請給我看你的登機證。

B : Sure, here you are.
　　在這裡！

A : OK. Welcome aboard.
　　好的！歡迎登機！

B : Thank you. Where is seat 22A?
　　謝謝！請問22A座位在哪裡？

A : This way, please. It's in the front of the cabin.
　　這邊請！就在機艙的前段。

B : Thanks.
　　謝謝！

找不到座位

I couldn't find my seat.

我找不到我的座位。

A : Well, where's my seat? 31...C...
　　嗯，我的座位在哪裡？31…C…

B : Welcome aboard. May I help you?
　　歡迎登機。需要我幫忙嗎？

A：Yes, I couldn't find my seat.
是的，我找不到我的座位。

B：Let me see your boarding pass.
讓我看看你的登機證。

A：Here is my boarding pass.
這是我的登機證。

 同義例句 -

例 Where is the seat 31C?
31C 的座位在哪裡？

例 Where is my seat?
我的座位在哪裡？

例 Could you show me where my seat is?
你能指出我的座位在哪裡嗎？

例 Could you tell me where my seat is?
你能告訴我我的座位在哪裡嗎？

確認機位　　　　　　　　　　　　　　　　MP3 021

My seat is 32L.
我的座位是 **32L**。

 實用會話 -

A：May I see your boarding pass?
請給我你的登機證。

B：Here you are. My seat is 32L.
在這裡。我的座位是 **32L**。

A：Go straight ahead, and you'll see it on the left side.
　　往前直走，你就會看到在左手邊。

B：Thank you.
　　謝謝！

相關例句 -

例 It's right over there, on the right aisle.
　　在那裡，在右邊走道。

例 It's a middle seat .
　　這是中間的座位。

例 It's a left middle seat.
　　這是中間靠左的座位。

例 It's a window seat on the left.
　　是在左邊靠窗戶的座位。

例 It's an aisle seat on your left side.
　　是在你的左手邊的靠走道座位。

詢問座位號碼

Is this 31C?

這是 **31C** 座位嗎？

實用會話 -

A：Excuse me.
　　請問一下！

B：Yes?
　　請說！

A：Is this 31C?
　　這是31C座位嗎？

B：No, this is 32C.
　　不是，這是32C。

A：Oh, I see. Thank you.
　　喔，我知道了！謝謝你！

B：No problem.
　　不客氣！

確認彼此的座位　　　　　　　　　　　　　

Is this your seat?

這是你的座位嗎？

實用會話 -

A：Is this your seat?
　　這是你的座位嗎？

B：Yes, I think so.
　　是啊，我想是吧！

A：My seat number is 31C, and I think this is it.
　　我的座位是31C，我覺得這是我的座位耶！

B：Oh, I'm sorry. My seat number is 26C. It's in the
　　next row.
　　喔，抱歉，我的座位是26C，在隔壁排。

A：It's OK.
　　沒關係！

有人錯坐在你的座位

This is my seat.

這是我的座位。

實用會話 --

A：Excuse me.
　　抱歉打擾一下。

B：Yes?
　　請說！

A：I'm afraid this is my seat.
　　這恐怕是我的座位。

B：Your seat? Oh, sorry, my mistake.
　　你的座位？喔，抱歉，我坐錯了。

A：It's OK.
　　沒關係！

同義例句 --

例 I'm afraid this is my seat.
　　這個恐怕是我的座位。

例 I'm afraid you have my seat.
　　你恐怕坐到我的座位了！

例 I think 32L is my seat.
　　我覺得 32L 是我的座位。

例 Someone has my seat.
　　有人坐到我的座位了！

例 Someone is already in my seat.
　　我的座位有人坐了！

想要換座位　 023

Can I change my seat?
我能不能換座位？

A：I know this is a full flight.
我知道班機客滿了。

B：Yes.
請說！

A：Can I change my seat?
我能不能換座位？

B：I'm afraid not, sir.
先生，很抱歉，恐怕辦不到耶！

同義例句--

例 Can you switch seats with me?
我可以和你換座位嗎？

例 Can we move to the smoking area?
我們能移到吸煙區嗎？

例 I'd like to move to the non-smoking area.
我想要換座位到非吸煙區。

例 I need to find somewhere else to sit.
我需要另外找個地方坐！

例 I don't care if it's a middle seat.
如果是在中間的座位也沒關係。

如何在飛機上放置行李

Where should I put my baggage?

我應該把我的行李放哪裡？

實用會話 --

A：Where should I put my baggage?
　　我應該把我的行李放哪裡？

B：You can store your baggage in the overhead cabinet.
　　你可以把你的行李放在上方的行李櫃裡。

A：Over here?
　　在這裡嗎？

B：Yes.
　　是的！

相關例句 --

例 Please help me put my baggage up.
　　請幫忙把我的袋子放上去。

例 Could you help me get my bags down?
　　可以幫忙拿我的袋子下來嗎？

例 Would you please put this bag in the overhead bin for me?
　　可以請你幫我把袋子放在頭頂的置物箱中嗎？

詢問空服員問題

Excuse me?
請問一下！

 實用會話 --

A : May I help you, madam?
　　女士，需要我幫忙嗎？

B : Would you put this in the overhead bin?
　　你可以幫我把這個放進頭頂上的櫃子裡嗎？

A : No problem, madam.
　　沒問題的，女士。

相關例句 --

例 How should I fasten my seat belt?
　　我要怎麼繫緊我的安全帶？

例 Where is the lavatory?
　　盥洗室在哪裡？

例 Can I recline my seat back now?
　　我現在可以將我的椅背往後靠嗎？

例 Can I pull the arm rests up?
　　我可以把扶手撐起來嗎？

例 May I smoke now?
　　我現在可以抽煙嗎？

不需要幫忙

I can arrange it by myself.

我可以自己來。

實用會話 --

A：I should place my bag in the...
　　我應該要把我的袋子放在⋯

B：Let me help you with it.
　　我來幫你。

A：I can arrange it by myself. Thank you.
　　我可以自己來。謝謝你！

同義例句 --

例 Don't worry about me.
　　不用擔心我。

例 I'm fine.
　　我很好。（不用幫我）

誰會說中文

 MP3 025

Does any one here speak Chinese?

這裡有人會說中文嗎？

實用會話 --

A：Does any one here speak Chinese?
　　這裡有人會說中文嗎？

B：Yes, sir, I am Taiwanese.
　　有的，先生，我是台灣人！

同義例句 --------------------------------------

例 Anyone here who can speak Chinese?
這裡有誰會說中文？

相關例句 --

例 Are there any native English speakers who can help me?
有母語是英文的人可以幫我嗎？

尋求空服員提供物品

May I have a blanket?

我能要一條毯子嗎？

實用會話 --

A：I feel cold. May I have a blanket?
　　我覺得冷！我能要一條毯子嗎？

B：Sure. Here you are.
　　好的。在這裡！

A：Thank you.
　　謝謝你！

B：Would you also like a pillow?
　　你要不要枕頭？

A：No, thanks.
　　不用了，謝謝！

同義例句 ---

例 May I have a pack of playing cards?
可以給我一副撲克牌嗎？

例 May I have a headset?
可以給我一副耳機嗎？

有沒有中文刊物　 MP3 026

Do you have any Chinese newspapers?

你們有中文報紙嗎？

實用會話 --

A：Excuse me.
請問一下！

B：Yes?
請說！

A：Do you have any Chinese newspapers?
你們有中文報紙嗎？

B：Sorry, sir, we don't. How about China Post?
很抱歉，先生，我們沒有。要不要看中國郵報呢？

A：Sure, I'd love to.
好啊！我願意。

同義例句 ---

例 Do you have any Chinese weekly magazine?
你們有中文週刊嗎？

詢問盥洗室是否使用中

Is this vacant?

(廁所)是空的嗎？

A：Excuse me. I need to go to the lavatory. Is this vacant?

請問一下，我需要去一趟洗手間。(廁所)是空的嗎？

B：No, it's occupied.

不是，(裡面)有人。

A：All right. I'll come back later.

好吧！我等一下再過來！

例 Is the lavatory now occupied or vacant?

廁所現在是有人在使用還是空的？

用餐時間

 027

What time will we have a meal served?

我們幾點用餐？

A：Excuse me.

請問一下！

B：Yes?

　　請説！

A：What time will we have a meal served?

　　我們幾點用餐？

B：About 30 minutes later. At 7 o'clock.

　　大約在三十分鐘後。在七點鐘。

A：I see. Thank you.

　　我瞭解了！謝謝！

同義例句--

例 I'm hungry.

　　我肚子餓了！

詢問有何種餐點

What do you have?

你們有什麼餐點？

實用會話--

A：What would you like for dinner, sir?

　　先生，晚餐你想吃什麼？

B：What do you have?

　　你們有什麼餐點？

A：We have beef and chicken.

　　我們有牛肉和雞肉。

B：I'd like to have beef. Thank you.

　　我要牛肉。謝謝！

A：Here you are. How about you, madam?
給你！女士，妳呢？

C：Chicken, please.
請給我雞肉！

 同義例句 --

例 Do you have instant noodles?
你們有泡麵嗎？

選擇餐點 **MP3** 028

I'd like beef, please.

我要吃牛肉，謝謝。

 實用會話 --

A：Excuse me, what would you like for dinner?
打擾一下，晚餐各位想吃什麼？

B：I'd like beef, please.
我要吃牛肉，謝謝。

A：Here you are, sir. How about you, madam?
給你，先生。女士，妳呢？

C：I'd like chicken.
我要吃雞肉。

A：Orange juice?
要喝柳橙汁嗎？

B：Yes, please.
好的，謝謝！

C：Make it two.
我也要。

素食餐點

Do you have a vegetarian meal?

你們有素食餐點嗎？

實用會話 --

A：What would you like for dinner, sir? Beef or chic-
　　ken?

　　先生，你晚餐要吃什麼？牛肉或雞肉？

B：Do you have a vegetarian meal?

　　你們有素食餐點嗎？

A：Yes, sir. We have rice and noodles. Which one do
　　you prefer?

　　有的，先生。我們有飯和麵，你喜歡哪一種？

B：I'd like to have noodles, please.

　　請給我麵。

同義例句 --

例 Is this a vegetarian meal?

　　這是素食餐點嗎？

詢問是否可以喝飲料

 MP3 029

May I have something to drink?

我能喝點飲料嗎？

A：May I help you?

　　需要我幫忙嗎？

B：May I have something to drink?
我能喝點飲料嗎？

A：What would you like to drink, sir?
先生，你想喝什麼呢？

B：Coke, please.
請給我可樂，謝謝！

A：OK. How about you, madam?
好的，女士，妳呢？

C：No, thanks.
不用，謝謝！

相關例句--

例 I'd like to have a glass of water.
我要喝一杯水。

例 I'd like to have cold drinks.
我要喝冷飲。

例 I want something cold.
我想喝點冷飲！

飲料的選擇

I'd like to have coffee.
我要喝咖啡。

實用會話--

A：What would you like to drink? Coffee or tea?
你想喝什麼呢？咖啡或茶？

B：I'd like to have coffee, please.
請給我咖啡。

A：No problem, sir. How about you, sir?
　　沒問題的，先生。先生，你呢？

C：Do you have any cold drinks?
　　你們有冷飲嗎？

A：We have apple juice and iced tea.
　　我們要蘋果汁和冰紅茶。

 同義例句 --

例 Coke, please.
　　請給我可樂！

例 Water, please.
　　請給我水！

例 Hot water, please.
　　請給我熱水！

例 Two coffees, please.
　　請給我兩杯咖啡。

要求再提供飲料　　　　　　　　　　**MP3 030**

Can I have another drink?

可以再給我一杯嗎？

 實用會話 --

A：Yes, sir?
　　先生，有什麼事嗎？

B：Can I have another drink?
　　可以再給我一杯嗎？

A：No problem, sir. I'll be right back with you.
沒問題的，先生，我馬上回來。

B：Thanks.
謝謝！

 同義例句 --

例 One more, please.
請再來一杯！

例 May I have some more coffee?
可以再多給我一些咖啡嗎？

例 May I have some more tea, please?
可以再多給我一些茶嗎？

例 Could you bring us two more coffees?
可以再多幫我們送兩杯咖啡過來嗎？

在飛機上生病

I have a headache.
我頭痛。

實用會話 --

A：Are you OK, sir?
先生，你還好吧？

B：I need a doctor.
我需要醫生。

A：What's the matter with you?
你怎麼了？

B：I don't know. I have a headache.
我不知道！我就是頭痛。

同義例句

例 I have a stomachache.
我胃痛。

例 I have a fever.
我發燒了。

在飛機上覺得不舒服 031

I'm not feeling well.

我覺得不舒服。

實用會話

A：Are you OK, sir? You look terrible.
先生，你還好嗎？你看起來氣色不太好耶！

B：I'm not feeling well.
我覺得不舒服。

A：Do you need a doctor?
你需要醫生嗎？

A：Yes, I think so.
好的，我覺得需要！

B：Wait a moment, please.
請稍等！

同義例句

例 I don't feel well.
我覺得不舒服！

例 I have a pain here.
我這裡痛！

例 I have a headache.
我頭痛！

請求提供醫藥服務
I'd like some medicine.
我需要一些藥。

實用會話 --

A：Sir, are you OK?
先生，你還好吧？

B：I don't know. I have a headache.
我不知道。我頭痛。

A：Do you need some medicine?
你需要一些藥嗎？

B：Yes, I'd like some medicine, please.
好的，我需要一些藥。

A：OK, sir. I'll be right back with you.
好的，先生，我馬上回來！

B：Thank you.
謝謝你。

A：Do you wanna take some aspirin, sir?
先生，你要吃點阿斯匹靈嗎？

有沒有暈機藥

May I have some medicine for airsickness?

我能要一些治療暈機的藥嗎?

A：Excuse me.

請問一下!

B：Yes?

請說!

A：May I have some medicine for airsickness?

我能要一些治療暈機的藥嗎?

B：Sure. Here you are.

當然可以!給你。

A：And may I have a glass of hot water?

可以給我一杯熱水嗎?

例 Please give me some airsickness pills.

請給我一些暈機藥。

抵達後行李提領

Where can I get my baggage?

我可以在哪裡提領我的行李？

實用會話 --

A：May I help you?
　　需要我幫忙嗎？

B：Where can I get my baggage?
　　我可以在哪裡提領我的行李？

A：Your baggage is on the conveyer.
　　你的行李在行李傳輸帶上。

同義例句 --

例 Is this the baggage claim area from Continental Airlines 364?
這是大陸航空 364 航班的行李提領處嗎？

例 Can I get my baggage now?
我可以現在提領我的行李嗎？

尋找行李提領區

Where is the baggage claim area?

哪裡是行李提領區？

A：May I help you?
　　需要我幫忙嗎？

B：Where is the baggage claim area?
哪裡是行李提領區？

A：Turn right, and you'll see it in front of you.
右轉你就會看到在你面前。

B：I see. Thank you.
我瞭解了，謝謝你。

A：No problem.
不客氣！

請求幫忙搬運行李

Could you help me get my baggage down?

可以幫我把我的行李拿下來嗎？

A：Excuse me, could you help me get my baggage down?
不好意思，你可以幫我把我的行李拿下來嗎？

B：Which one?
哪一個？

A：The red one, please.
紅色的那個，謝謝！

B：No problem. Here you are.
沒問題！給你！

A：Thank you so much.
非常感謝你。

B：You're welcome.
不客氣！

行李被誤拿 MP3 034

That is my baggage.
那是我的行李。

實用會話

A：Excuse me, sir, but that is my baggage.
先生，抱歉，那是我的行李。

B：Which one?
哪一個？

A：The red one is mine. This is my baggage claim tag.
那個紅色的是我的！這是我的行李牌。

B：Which one? The red one with wheels?
哪一個？是紅色有輪子的這個嗎？

A：Yes, it is.
對，就是它。

B：Oh, sorry.
喔，抱歉！

A：It's OK.
沒關係！

同義例句

例 Excuse me, but you took my suitcase.
抱歉，你拿了我的行李。

發覺行李遺失

I can't find my baggage.

我找不到我的行李。

 實用會話

A：May I help you?
　　需要我幫忙嗎？

B：I can't find my baggage. What can I do?
　　我找不到我的行李。我應該怎麼辦？

A：OK. I'll see what I can do for you.
　　好的！我看看能幫上什麼忙。

B：Thank you so much.
　　非常謝謝你！

A：No problem.
　　不客氣！

同義例句

例 I don't see my baggage.
　　我沒有看見我的行李。

例 I think I've lost my baggage.
　　我想我遺失行李了！

尋找行李遺失申報處

 MP3 035

Where is the Lost Baggage Service?

「行李遺失服務處」在哪裡？

實用會話

A：May I help you?
　　需要我幫忙嗎？

B：Yes. Where is the Lost Baggage Service?
　　是的！「行李遺失服務處」在哪裡？

A：It's over there.
　　在那裡。

B：Oh, I see. Thank you.
　　喔，我瞭解！謝謝！

A：Sure thing.
　　不客氣！

同義例句

例 Where can I find the Lost Baggage Service?
　　我可以在哪裡找到「行李遺失服務處」？

例 Do you know where the Lost Baggage Service is?
　　你知道「行李遺失服務處」在哪裡嗎？

行李遺失的數量

We may have lost some baggage.

我們可能遺失一些行李了！

實用會話 --

A：We may have lost some baggage.
　　我們可能遺失一些行李了！

B：How many bags are missing?
　　少了幾件袋子？

A：There are two.
　　(總共)有兩件。

B：Please fill out this claim form.
　　請填這張申訴表格。

同義例句 --

例 One of my bags hasn't come.
　　我有一件行李沒有出來。

例 I'm missing three suitcases.
　　我少了三件行李。

例 I think two pieces of my baggage have been lost.
　　我覺得我的兩件行李遺失了。

036

遺失行李的外觀

My baggage is black.

我的行李是黑色的。

實用會話 --

A：Can you tell me the features of your baggage?
能形容一下你的行李的外觀嗎？

B：It's medium-sized.
中等尺寸。

A：What's the color?
什麼顏色？

B：It's black.
是黑色的。

A：OK, let me check...
好的，我確認一下…

同義例句 --

例 They are green and with wheels.
它們都是綠色有輪子的。

通關時查驗證件

This is my passport and visa.

這是我的護照和簽證。

實用會話 --

A：May I see your passport and visa, please?
請給我你的護照和簽證。

B：This is my passport and visa.
這是我的護照和簽證。

例 Sure. Here you are.
當然可以。在這裡。

例 I couldn't find my visa.
我找不到我的簽證。

通關盤查   MP3 037

Are you traveling alone?
自己來旅遊的嗎？

實用會話

A：Are you traveling alone or with someone?
自己來旅遊或是和誰一起來的嗎？

B：Yes, I am alone.
是的，我一個人（來的）。

A：Sir, your air ticket indicates that you're traveling with two other passengers.
先生，你的機票顯示你有兩位同行的伙伴。

B：How come I have two other buddies go with me? Where are they?
怎麼我會有兩位同行的伙伴？他們在哪裡？

A：Sorry, sir. There is a restriction for your ticket. You have to check-in with the other two members. So, you better find the other two buddies, otherwise our airline can't let you check-in.

抱歉，先生，這是你機票的限制。你要和其他兩位一起登機報到。所以你最好趕緊找到他們，不然我無法讓你登機報到。

同義例句 --

例 I'm with my parents.
　　我和我父母一起來的。

例 I'm with a travel tour.
　　我是跟團的。

回答入境的原因

It's for business.

(我)是來出差的。

實用會話 --

A：What's the purpose of your visit?
　　你此行的目的是什麼？

B：It's for business.
　　(我)是來出差的。

同義例句 --

例 I'm here for sightseeing.
　　我來這裡觀光。

例 I'm here for touring.
　　我來這裡旅行。

例 I'm here for studies.
我來這裡唸書的。

例 Just touring.
只是旅遊。

例 To see my friends.
來探望我的朋友！

過境 038

I'm just passing through.

我只是過境。

實用會話 --------------------------------

A：What's the purpose of your visit?
此行的目的為何？

B：I'm just passing through.
我只是過境。

A：Do you have your return ticket?
你有回程機票嗎？

B：Yes. Here it is.
有，在這裡！

A：Okay. Here is your passport. Have a nice trip.
好的！你的護照還你。祝你旅途愉快。

同義例句 --------------------------------

例 I'm leaving for New York tonight.
我今晚要過境到紐約。

例 I'm on my way to Seattle.
我要過境去西雅圖。

預計停留的時間

I'll stay here for 10 days.

我會在這裡留十天。

A：How long are you going to stay?
你要停留多久？

B：I'll stay here for 10 days.
我會在這裡停留十天。

例 10 days.
十天！

例 It's about 10 days.
大概十天。

例 I'll stay here for about 10 days.
我大約會在這裡停留十天。

例 I'm planning to stay here for 10 days.
我打算要在這裡停留十天。

相關例句 --

例 I'll stay here for 3 weeks.
我會在這裡停留三個星期。

回答住宿的問題 MP3 039

I'm going to stay at Four Seasons Hotel.

我會住在四季飯店。

A：Where are you going to stay during this time?
這段時間你會在哪裡住宿？

B：I'm going to stay at Four Seasons Hotel.
我會住在四季飯店。

A：OK. Here is your passport and visa. Have a nice trip.
好的，這是你的護照和簽證。祝你旅途愉快！

同義例句 --

例 Four Seasons Hotel.
(住在)四季飯店。

例 I'll be staying at Four Seasons Hotel.
我會住宿在四季飯店。

例 I'm going to stay in a hotel.
我會住飯店。

相關例句 --

例 I'm going to stay at my aunt's house.
我要住在我姑姑家。

例 I will stay with my friends.
我會住在我朋友家。

檢查攜帶的隨身物品

Those are just personal belongings.

這些都只是個人用品。

實用會話 ---

A：Do you have any metal items in your bag?
你的袋子裡有任何的金屬物品嗎？

B：No, I don't.
沒有，我沒有！

A：Why do you take them with you?
你為什麼帶這些東西？

B：Those are just personal belongings.
這些都只是個人用品。

A：OK. Have a nice trip.
好！祝你旅途愉快！

同義例句 ---

例 Those medicines are prepared for this tour.
這些藥物是為了這趟旅行而準備的。

例 They are just some souvenirs.
它們只是一些紀念品。

例 Personal stuff.
私人物品。

解釋行李內的物品　**MP3 040**

They are presents for my parents.
這是給我父母的禮物。

 -

A：Open your baggage, please.
　　請打開你的行李。

B：OK. Here you are.
　　好的，請看。

A：What are these?
　　這些是什麼？

B：They are presents for my parents.
　　這是給我父母的禮物。

相關例句 -

例 Personal stuff.
　 私人物品。

例 They are gifts for my friends.
　 他們是要給我朋友的禮物！

例 Those are presents for my family.
　 是給我家人的禮物。

例 Those medicines are prepared for this tour.
　 那些藥物是為了這趟旅行而準備的。

入境時是否要申報物品

Do you have anything to declare?
有沒有要申報的物品？

 實用會話 --

A：Are you carrying any drugs or illegal items?
你有攜帶任何的毒品或違法物品嗎？

B：No, sir.
長官，沒有。

A：Do you have anything to declare?
有沒有要申報的物品？

B：Yes, there are 6 bottles of wine.
有的，有六瓶酒要申報。

A：OK. Please fill up this declaration.
好的！請填申報單。

相關例句 --

例 I have a carton of cigarettes.
我有一條香菸要申報。

例 I have 6 bottles of wine to declare.
我有六瓶酒要申報。

例 I have nothing to declare.
我沒有物品要申報。

何處可以兌換貨幣　MP3 041

Where is the Currency Exchange?

「錢幣兌換處」在哪裡？

實用會話

A：May I help you?
需要我幫忙嗎？

B：Yes. Where is the Currency Exchange?
是的。「錢幣兌換處」在哪裡？

A：Turn left, and you'll see it.
左轉你就會看到。

同義例句

例 Where can I exchange money?
我可以到哪裡兌換錢幣？

例 Where can I find a bank around here?
這附近哪裡有銀行？

例 Do you know where I can get this changed?
你知道我可以在哪裡換開這個嗎？

大鈔兌換成零錢

I'd like to exchange money.

我要兌換錢幣。

實用會話

A：Excuse me.
打擾一下！

B：May I help you?
需要我幫忙嗎？

A：I'd like to exchange money.
我要兌換錢幣。

B：How much would you like to exchange?
要換成多少？

同義例句 -

例 Could you break this $100?
可以找開這張一百元嗎？

例 I'd like to break this $1,000 bill.
我要換開這一張一千元。

例 Can you break this bill?
可以將這張紙鈔換成零錢嗎？

例 Would you please break this $200?
請將二百元換成零錢。

例 Can you break this into small money?
可以兌換成小鈔嗎？

兌換為零錢的數目   MP3 042

Can you exchange a dollar for ten dimes?

能把一美元換成十個一角的銀幣嗎？

 實用會話 -

A：Can you make me change for this bill?
這張鈔票能找得開嗎？

B：How much do you want to exchange?
你想兌換多少？

A：Let's see... Can you exchange a dollar for ten dimes?
我想想…你能把一美元換成十個一角的銀幣嗎？

同義例句 --

例 Could you give me some small change with it?
能把這些兌換為小面額零錢嗎？

例 I want to break this 200 dollars into 4 twenties, 3 tens and the rest in coins.
我想要將兩百元兌換成四張二十元、三張十元，剩下的是硬幣。

例 Could you include some small change?
可以包括一些零錢嗎？

幣值匯率

What's the exchange rate?

匯率是多少？

實用會話 --

A：What's the exchange rate?
匯率是多少？

B：The exchange rate from U.S. dollar to New Taiwan dollar is thirty-five point five.
現在美金兌換成新台幣的匯率是卅五點五。

同義例句 --

例 What is the exchange rate now?
現在的匯率是多少？

例 Could you tell me the procedures and the exchange rate?
你能告訴我辦理的手續和匯率嗎？

兌換幣值

Could you change this into U.S. dollars?

可以把這個兌換為美元嗎？

實用會話 ---

A：What currency do you want to convert from?
你想要用哪一種貨幣兌換？

B：Could you change this into U.S. dollars?
可以把這個兌換為美元嗎？

A：Sure. Here is $147.
當然可以！這裡是一百四十七元。

同義例句 ---

例 How much in dollars is that?
（兌換）美元是多少？

例 I'd like to change these dollars into U.S. dollars.
我要把這些錢兌換成美金。

例 I'd like to exchange some U.S. dollars to German Marks.
我要把一些美金兌換成德國馬克。

例 I'd like to change NT$10,000 into U.S. dollars.
我要把一萬元台幣換成美金。

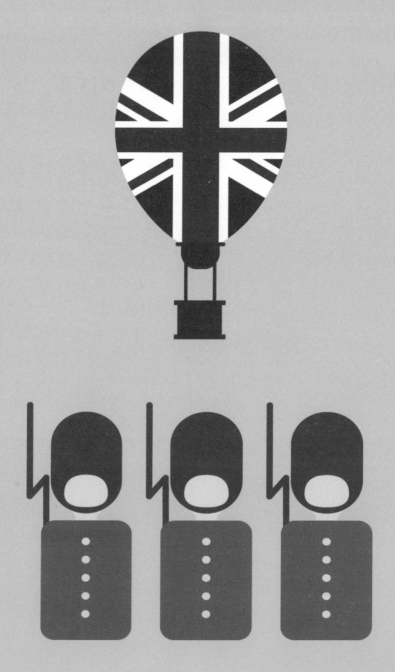

Chapter 3

住宿

English Travel around the World

事先預約住宿 **MP3 044**

I'm interested in booking a room for next weekend.

我想要預訂下週末的住宿。

A：Thanks for calling Snow Hotel. Maria speaking.
白雪飯店你好，我是瑪莉亞。

B：Hello. I'm interested in booking a room for next weekend.
你好，我想要預訂下週末的住宿。

A：I'm afraid we're totally booked for that weekend.
抱歉，那個週末我們已經客滿了。

B：Well, what about the weekend after that?
嗯，那個週末之後呢？

A：So... Friday the seventeenth?
所以是…17日的星期五嗎？

B：Yes. Friday and Saturday.
對，星期五和星期六。

協調訂房

We recommend that you make a reservation.

我們建議你先預約。

實用會話

A：Do you still have a vacancy for two?
你們還有兩人房的空房嗎？

B：How long will you be staying?
你要住多久？

A：From this Tuesday to Friday.
從這個星期二到星期五。

B：Lets see... It looks like we have a few vacancies left.
我看看⋯看來我們還有一些空房。

A：That's great.
太好了！

B：We recommend that you make a reservation, though. It's still considered peak season then.
我們建議你還是先預約，現在還是旺季。

A：OK, I'll book a double room.
好，我要訂一間雙人房。

電話預約住宿

I'll book a double room.

我要預定一間雙人房。

實用會話 --

A：We recommend that you make a reservation.
我們建議你先預約。

B：No problem.
好啊！

A：But we do require a fifty dollar credit card deposit to hold the room. You can cancel up to five days in advance and we will refund your deposit.
可是我們需要五十元的信用卡預約付款。你可以在五天前取消訂房，我們也會退款。

B：Great, I'll book a double room. I'll call you right back. I have to find my credit card.
太好了！我要預定一間雙人房。我等一下回你電話，我找一下我的信用卡。

飯店的設施

Will your outdoor pool be closed next week?

下星期你們的戶外游泳池會關閉嗎？

實用會話 --

A：Hi, I'd like to book a double room.
嗨，我要預訂一間雙人房。

B：OK.
好的！

A：Will your outdoor pool be closed next week?
下星期你們的戶外游泳池會關閉嗎？

B：That's right.
對。

A：I see.
我知道了！

B：Oh, and just to let you know... our indoor pool is open.
喔，讓你知道一下，我們的室內游泳池有開放。

A：I see. Thanks.
我知道了！謝謝！

一家人的訂房 **MP3 046**

We're a family of four.
我們是一家四人。

實用會話 --

A：Do you have any rooms with two double beds? We're a family of four.
你們有兩張雙人床的房間嗎？我們是一家四人。

B：Yes, all of our rooms have two double beds.
有的，我們都是兩張雙人床房間。

A：Great. How much is the rate?
太好了！要多少錢？

B：The rate for that weekend is 129 dollars a night.
週末一晚的費用是一百廿九元。

A：That's reasonable.
很合理。

額外費用

One of my daughters might be bringing a friend.

我的一個女兒可能會帶朋友來過夜。

實用會話 --

A：Do you have any rooms with a king bed?
你們有加大床鋪的房間嗎？

B：Yes, we do.
有的，我們有！

A：Great. I'll book 2 double rooms.
太好了！我要訂兩間雙人房！

B：Sure. Please fill up this form.
好的！請填寫這份表格。

A：And do you have cots? One of my daughters might be bringing a friend.
還有你們可以加床嗎？我的一個女兒可能會帶朋友來過夜。

B：We do, but we also charge an extra ten dollars per person for any family with over four people. The cot is free.
我們有，但是每個人我們要酌收十元。床鋪是免費的。

詢問空房   047

Do you have a twin-bedded room?

你們有兩張單人床的房間嗎？

A：May I help you?
　　需要我幫忙嗎？

B：Do you have a twin-bedded room?
　　你們有兩張單人床的房間嗎？

A：Yes, we do.
　　是的，我們有。

B：I'll take it.
　　我要訂。

A：How long will you be staying?
　　你要住多久？

同義例句 ---

例 Any rooms for two?
　　有給兩人住的房間嗎？

例 Do you have any vanancies?
　　你們有空房嗎？

例 We'd like a room for two.
　　我們要雙人的房間。

例 Do you still have a vacancy?
　　你們還有空房嗎？

詢問房間的種類

Do you have a single room on a lower floor?

你們有低樓層的單人房嗎？

實用會話 --

A：May I help you?
需要我幫忙嗎？

B：Do you have a single room on a lower floor?
你們有低樓層的單人房嗎？

A：No, but we have a double on the second floor.
沒有，但是我們有一間在二樓的雙人房。

相關例句 --

例 Do you have a single room?
你們有單人房嗎？

例 Do you have a double room?
你們有雙人房嗎？

例 Do you have a double room with twin beds?
你們有兩張單人床的雙人房嗎？

例 Do you have any rooms with a king bed?
你們有加大床鋪的房間嗎？

投宿的人數

We'd like a room for two.

我們要雙人的房間。

實用會話

A：Would you like a double room or two single rooms?
你要雙人房還是二間單人房？

B：We'd like a room for two.
我們要雙人的房間。

A：OK. How about single separate beds?
好的！兩張分開的單人床房間可以嗎？

B：Sure, I'll take it.
好，我就要這個！

A：And it's on the third floor.
還有這是在三樓。

B：That would be fine.
很好。

同義例句

例 I'd like a room for one.
我要一間單人房。

例 I'd like a room for two with separate beds.
我要一間有兩張床的雙人房間。

住宿的天數

I plan to stay here for two nights.

我計畫要在這裡住兩晚。

 實用會話 -

A：Do you have a single room?
你們有單人房嗎？

B：How many nights will you stay?
你想要住幾晚？

A：I plan to stay here for two nights.
我計畫要在這裡住兩晚。

B：OK! May I have your name, please?
好的！請問你的大名？

A：My name is David Smith.
我是大衛・史密斯。

 同義例句 -

例 I'm going to stay for two nights.
我要住兩晚。

詢問可供住兩晚的空房

MP3 049

Do you have a single room for 2 nights?

你們有單人房可以住兩晚嗎？

A：May I help you?
　　需要我幫忙嗎？

B：Do you have a single room for 2 nights?
　　你們有單人房可以住兩晚嗎？

A：We only have a small suite.
　　我們只有一個小套房。

B：OK, I'll take it.
　　好，我就要這個！

A：No problem, sir. Do you have any ID on you?
　　沒問題的，先生。你有帶證件嗎？

B：Yes, here is my passport.
　　有的，這是我的護照。

長時間的住宿需求

Do you have a double room from Monday to Friday?

你們還有星期一到星期五的雙人房嗎?

實用會話 --

A：May I help you?
　　需要我幫忙嗎?

B：Yes. Do you have a double room from Monday to Friday?
　　是的。你們還有星期一到星期五的雙人房嗎?

A：No, but I can let you have one until Wednesday.
　　沒有,但是我可以給你一間住到星期三的雙人房。

B：OK, I'll take it.
　　好,我就要這個!

A：No problem, sir. May I have your passport, please?
　　沒問題的,先生!請給我你的護照!

B：Here you are.
　　在這裡!

A：Thanks. Please fill in the form.
　　謝謝!請填寫這個表格。

旅館客滿

We're all booked up.

我們全部客滿了。

A：May I help you?
　　需要我幫忙嗎？

B：Do you have a twin available?
　　你們有兩張單人床的房間嗎？

A：I'm sorry, sir, but we're all booked up.
　　抱歉，先生，我們全部客滿了。

相關例句--

例 I'm afraid we are booked that weekend.
　那個星期恐怕都已經客滿了！

例 There are only a few vacancies left.
　只有剩下一些空房。

其他的訂房選擇

I can let you have two single rooms.

我可以讓你有兩間單人房。

A：Do you have a double room?
　　你們有雙人床的房間嗎？

B：No, but I can let you have two single rooms.
沒有，但是我可以讓你有兩間單人房。

A：Are they on the lower floor?
是在低樓層嗎？

B：Let's see... yes, they are on the second floor.
我看看…是的，都在二樓！

預約訂房　

Can I reserve a double room next week?

我可以預訂下星期的一間雙人房嗎？

實用會話 --

A：May I help you?
需要我幫忙嗎？

B：Yes. Can I reserve a double room next week?
是的。我可以預訂下星期的一間雙人房嗎？

A：No problem, sir.
沒問題的，先生！

同義例句 --

例 I'd like to book a single room tonight.
我要預約今晚的一間單人房。

決定要訂房

I'll take it.

我要訂。

實用會話 --

A：Do you have any rooms for two?
你們有可以住兩人的房間嗎？

B：Yes. We have a double room available.
有的，我們有一個雙人床房間。

A：OK. I'll take it.
好，我要訂。

B：OK, sir. May I have your passport?
好的，先生，請給我看你的護照。

A：Sure, here you are.
好的，在這裡！

詢問房價

 MP3 052

How much is it?

(住宿)要多少錢？

實用會話 --

A：How much is it?
(住宿)要多少錢？

B：5 hundred dollars per night, plus tax.
含稅一晚要五百元。

(同)(義)(例)(句) ------------------------------------

例 How much per night?

(住宿)一晚要多少錢？

例 How much would it be?

要多少錢？

例 What's the rate?

要多少錢？

例 What's the daily rate?

每天的費用是多少？

例 How much should I pay for a week?

一個星期得付多少錢？

例 How much for a single room?

單人房多少錢？

(相)(關)(例)(句) ------------------------------------

例 Do you have any cheaper rooms?

你們有便宜一點的房間嗎？

房價包括的項目

Are there any meals included?

有包括餐點嗎？

(實)(用)(會)(話) ------------------------------------

A：Are there any meals included?

有包括餐點嗎？

B：Yes, sir. It includes breakfast.

有的，先生，有包含早餐。

A：When is breakfast served?
早餐什麼時候供應？

B：It's from 6 am until 10 am.
從早上六點到九點鐘。

A：I see, thank you.
我知道了！謝謝！

B：You're welcome.
不客氣！

（同）（義）（例）（句）--

例 Does it include tax?
有含稅嗎？

房價包括早餐   MP3 053

$80 a night, including breakfast.

一晚要八十元，包含早餐。

（實）（用）（會）（話）--

A：How much will it be?
要多少錢？

B：$80 a night, including breakfast.
一晚要八十元，包含早餐。

A：Oh, it's too expensive.
喔，太貴了！

（同）（義）（例）（句）--

例 Does the room rate include breakfast?
住宿費有包括早餐嗎？

登記住宿

I'd like to check in.

我要登記住宿。

實用會話 --

A：May I help you, sir?
　　先生，需要我幫忙嗎？

B：I'd like to check in.
　　我要登記住宿。

A：OK, sir, may I have your name?
　　好的，先生，請問你的大名？

B：Sure. My name is David Jones.
　　有！我的名字是大衛‧瓊斯。

同義例句 --

例 I have a reservation for 4 nights.
　　我已訂了四天的住宿。

例 Here is the confirmation slip.
　　這是確認單。

可以登記住宿的時間

What time can I check in?

我什麼時候可以登記住宿？

實用會話 --

A：What time can I check in?
　　我什麼時候可以登記住宿？

B：Anytime after 11 am.
　　早上十一點鐘之後都可以。

A：Oh, it's only nine thirty now.
　　喔，現在才九點半。

C：Maybe we can go to the museum.
　　也許我們可以去博物館。

A：It sounds good.
　　聽起來不錯！

同義例句 --

例 When is the check-in time?
　 什麼時候可以登記住宿？

詢問是否預約住宿

Did you make a reservation?

有預約住宿嗎？

A：Did you make a reservation?
　　有預約住宿嗎？

B：Yes, I have a reservation. My name is Tom Jones.
有的，我有預約訂房。我的名字是湯姆‧瓊斯。

例 No, I didn't make a reservation.
沒有，我沒有預約。

有預約訂房

Here is the confirmation slip.

這是我的確認單。

實用會話 --

A：I had a reservation at the airport today.
我今天在機場有預約訂房。

B：I'm sorry, sir, I couldn't find your name.
先生，很抱歉，我找不到你的名字。

A：Here is the confirmation slip.
這是我的確認單。

B：Thank you, sir.
謝謝你，先生。

相關例句 --

例 I made a reservation in Taiwan last week.
我上週在台灣有預約訂房。

房間的樓層

What's the floor?

在幾樓？

A：Here is your key card.
這是(房間)鑰匙卡片。

B：Thank you. What's the floor?
謝謝！在幾樓？

A：On the third floor, sir.
在三樓，先生。

B：OK. Excuse me, but where is the elevator?
好！請問一下，電梯在哪裡？

A：Turn right and you'll see it on your right side.
右轉就會看到在你的右手邊。

增加住宿天數

I want to stay for two more nights.

我想要再多住二晚。

A：May I help you?
需要我幫忙嗎？

B：I missed my plane this morning, so I want to stay
for two more nights.
我錯過今早的飛機了，所以我想要再多住二晚。

A：No problem, sir. May I have your name?
沒問題的，先生，請問你的大名？

B：David Smith.
大衛‧史密斯。

A：Let's see... OK, sir, you can stay two more until this Friday.
我看看…好的，先生，你可以在這裡多住兩晚直到星期五。

B：Thank you so much.
感謝你！

推薦其他旅館

Could you recommend another hotel?

你可以推薦另一個旅館嗎？

實用會話 --

A：Sorry, sir, but we're all booked up tonight.
抱歉，先生，我們今晚都客滿了！

B：It's OK. But could you recommend another hotel?
沒關係！但是你可以推薦其他的旅館嗎？

A：Yes. There is another hotel at the First Street.
好的。在第一街有另一家旅館。

同義例句 --

例 Are there any hotels around here?
這附近還有沒有旅館？

例 Are there any hotels nearby?
這附近還有沒有旅館？

旅館用餐 057

What time is breakfast served?

早餐什麼時候供應？

A：This is your breakfast coupon.
這是你的早餐券。

B：Thanks.
謝謝！

A：You're welcome.
不客氣！

B：By the way, what time is breakfast served?
對了，早餐什麼時候供應？

A：It's from 7 am until 10 am.
從早上七點到十點鐘。

相關例句

例 Where should I go to for breakfast?
我應該去哪裡用早餐？

沒有早餐券

I lost my breakfast coupon.

我把早餐券弄丟了。

A：I lost my breakfast coupon.
　　我把早餐券弄丟了。

B：It doesn't matter. Just tell me your room number.
　　沒關係。只要告訴我你的房號就好。

同義例句

例 I forgot to bring breakfast coupons with me.
　　我忘了帶早餐券。

表明身分及房號

MP3 058

I'm Jack Smith of Room 111.

我是 111 號房的傑克‧史密斯。

實用會話

A：What's your room number?
　　你的房號是幾號？

B：I'm Jack Smith of Room 111.
　　我是 111 號房的傑克‧史密斯。

相關例句

例 This is Room 502.
　　這是 502 號房。

例 My room number is 145.
我的房間號碼是 145。

請求提供房間鑰匙

Room 502 Key, please.

請給我 **502** 房號的鑰匙。

A：Room 502 Key, please.
　　請給我502房號的鑰匙。

B：Here you are, sir.
　　先生，在這裡。

同義例句 ---

例 Key to Room 502, please.
我要拿房號 502 的鑰匙。

例 My room number is 502. Key, please.
我的房間號碼是 502。請給我鑰匙。

早上叫醒服務

Can I have a morning call tomorrow?

我能設定明天早上叫醒的服務嗎？

實用會話 ---

A：Can I have a morning call tomorrow?
　　我能要求明天早上叫醒的服務嗎？

B：Of course you can. What time do you want?
　　當然可以。你想要什麼時間（叫醒）？

A：Seven, please.
　　七點鐘，謝謝！

B：Yes, sir.
　　好的，先生。

同義例句 --

例 Give me a wake-up call at seven, please.
　　請在七點鐘打電話叫醒我。

例 I'd like a wake-up call every morning.
　　我每一天都要早上叫醒(的服務)。

例 I'd like to have a wake-up call at 8 am.
　　我要早上八點鐘的電話叫醒服務。

例 Could I have a morning call, please?
　　我能有早上叫醒的服務嗎？

客房送餐服務

I'd like to order some coffee and toast.

我要點一些咖啡和吐司！

實用會話 --

A：Room service. May I help you, sir?
　　客房服務，先生，有什麼需要我服務的？

B：I'd like to order some coffee and toast, please.
　　我要點一些咖啡和吐司，麻煩你囉！

相關例句 --

例 I'd like to order room service, please.
我要食物送到房間的服務。

例 Will you send up two cups of coffee, please?
請你送兩杯咖啡上來，謝謝！

例 Please bring me a pot of tea.
請帶給我一壺茶。

例 Would you bring us a bottle of champagne?
你能帶一瓶香檳給我們嗎？

例 Let's see, and I want a beef sandwich.
我想想，還有我要一份牛肉三明治。

餐食送到房間   MP3 060

Who is it?

哪一位？（有人敲門時）

實用會話 --

A：Yes, this is room service. How may I help you?
你好，這是客房服務，需要我幫忙嗎？

B：This is David Smith of room 912. Could you bring
me some hot tea?
我是912號房的大衛‧史密斯，可以幫我送一點熱茶過來嗎？

A：Absolutely, Mr. Smith. Right away.
沒問題，史密斯先生。馬上過去。

B：Who is it?
哪一位？（有人敲門時）

C：Room service.
　　客房服務。

B：Wait a moment, please.
　　請稍等。

客房服務

I'd like an extra pillow for Room 504.

我要在 **504** 房多加一個枕頭。

實用會話 ---

A：May I help you, sir?
　　先生，有什麼需要我服務的？

B：I'd like an extra pillow for Room 504.
　　我要在504房多加一個枕頭。

A：No problem, sir. Do you need anything else?
　　沒問題的，先生。還有其他需要嗎？

同義例句 ---

例 I can't find any towels in my room.
　　我的房裡沒有毛巾。

例 Could you bring some towels right now?
　　請你馬上送幾條毛巾過來好嗎？

要求多加一張床

 MP3 061

I'd like an extra cot for Room 106.

我要在 **106** 房多加一張床。

A：I'd like an extra cot for Room 106.
　　我要在106房多加一張床。

B：Yes, sir, we'll arrange it for you right away.
　　好的，先生，我們會盡快為你安排。

A：How much does it charge?
　　這要收多少錢？

B：It's $120 for each extra cot. We'll charge you when you check out.
　　每加一張床要一百廿元。我們會在你退房時收費。

衣物送洗

Do you have the laundry service?

你們有洗衣服務嗎？

A：Do you have the laundry service?
　　你們有洗衣服務嗎？

B：Yes, we do. Please put it in the plastic bag and leave it on the bed.
　　有的，我們有。請放在塑膠袋裡，然後放在床上。

同義例句 --

例 I'd like to have my suit pressed.
我要衣服的熨燙服務。

例 I have some laundry.
我有一些衣服要送洗。

例 I'd like to send my suit to the cleaners.
我要把我的西裝送洗。

拿回送洗的衣物 062

When can I have my suit returned?

我什麼時候可以取回我的西裝？

 實用會話 --

A：From what time do you accept the laundry?
你們從什麼時候開始受理送洗的衣物？

B：From 8 am until 10 pm.
從早上八點到晚上十點鐘。

A：When can I have my suit returned?
我什麼時候可以取回我的西裝？

B：By this afternoon.
下午之前就可以。

同義例句 --

例 I haven't gotten the coat back that I sent to the cleaners yesterday.
我昨天送洗的外套還沒送回來。

旅館設施出問題

My phone is out of order.

我的電話故障了。

 實用會話 ---

A：May I help you?
　　需要我幫忙嗎？

B：Yes, my phone is out of order.
　　是的，我的電話故障了。

相關例句 ---

例 The air conditioner makes a funny noise.
　　空調有奇怪的聲音。

例 The dryer doesn't work.
　　吹風機壞了。

例 There is no hot water in my room.
　　我的房間裡沒有熱水。

例 There is something wrong with the toilet.
　　馬桶有點問題。

例 The toilet doesn't flush.
　　馬桶不能沖水了。

例 The bulb burnt out.
　　燈泡燒壞了！

例 The water doesn't drain.
　　水流不出來。

例 We are out of the toilet paper.
　　我們沒有衛生紙了。

在房間內打外線電話　 **063**

How do I call a number outside this hotel?

我要怎麼從旅館撥外線出去？

實用會話 -

A：How do I call a number outside this hotel?
　　我要怎麼從旅館撥外線出去？

B：Dial 9 first, and then the phone number.
　　先撥九，再來是(撥)電話號碼。

同義例句 -

例 I'd like to place an overseas call.
　　我要撥打國際電話。

例 Is this coin all right for telephones?
　　這個硬幣可以打電話嗎？

例 Could you connect me with the telephone directory assistance?
　　可以幫我接查號台嗎？

詢問退房時間

When is the check-out time?

退房的時間是什麼時候？

 -

A：When is the check-out time?
　　退房的時間是什麼時候？

B：Before 11 am.
　　早上十一點鐘之前。

A：I see, thank you.
　　我知道了，謝謝你！

B：You're welcome.
　　不客氣！

辦理退房　　　　　　　　　　　　　　　　MP3 064

Check out, please.

請結帳。

實用會話--

A：Check out, please.
　　請結帳。

B：Yes, sir. Just a moment, please.
　　好的，先生。請稍等！

A：Sure.
　　好的。

B：Here is your bill, sir.
　　先生，這是你的帳單。

A：Oh, I'm afraid there is something wrong with the
　　bill.
　　喔，帳單好像有點問題耶！

同義例句--

例 I'd like to check out.
　　我要結帳。

結帳

How much does it charge?

這要收多少錢？

A：How much does it charge?
　　這要收多少錢？

B：Your bill is twenty hundred dollars.
　　你的帳單是兩千元。

A：Are there any additional charges?
　　是否有其他附加費用？

A：Yes, it includes the room service and an extra cot.
　　有的，有包括客房服務和加床費用。

B：Oh, I see.
　　喔，我知道了！

相關例句 --

例 Put it on my hotel bill, please.
　　請算在我的住宿費裡。

付帳方式

MP3 065

I'll pay cash.

我會付現金。

A：How would you like to pay it, sir?
　　先生，你要怎麼結帳呢？

B：I'll pay cash.
　　我會付現金。

(相)(關)(例)(句)--

例 I'll pay credit card.
　　我會用信用卡(付)。

例 Can I pay with a traveler's check?
　　我可以用旅行支票付款嗎？

特定的信用卡付款

Do you accept credit cards?

你們接受信用卡付款嗎？

(實)(用)(會)(話)--

A：Do you accept credit cards?
　　你們接受信用卡付款嗎？

B：Yes, we do.
　　是的，我們有。

(同)(義)(例)(句)--

例 Can I use VISA?
　　我可以用 VISA 卡嗎？

例 Do you take MasterCard?
　　你們接受萬事達卡嗎？

(相)(關)(例)(句)--

例 Sorry, we only accept cash.
　　抱歉，我們只收現金。

帳單有問題

There is something wrong with the bill.

帳單有點問題。

A：I'm afraid there is something wrong with the bill.
這帳單恐怕有點問題吧！

B：Sorry, sir. Let me take a look.
抱歉，先生。我看一看。

同義例句

例 Something wrong with the bill.
帳單有點問題。

相關例句

例 Are the service charges and tax included?
是否包括服務費和稅金？

和櫃臺互動

I'd like to change my room.

我想換房間。

A：How may I help you, sir?
先生，需要我幫忙嗎？

B：I'd like to change my room.
　　我想換房間。

A：What's wrong, sir?
　　先生，怎麼了？

相關例句 --

例 Where is the locker?
　　寄物櫃在哪裡？

例 Do I have any messages?
　　我有任何的留言嗎？

例 I have lost my room key.
　　我遺失我的房間鑰匙了。

例 I locked myself out.
　　我把自己反鎖在外面。

例 Could you store my baggage?
　　請你幫我保管行李好嗎？

例 I'd like to pick up my baggage.
　　我要拿行李。

例 Could you call a taxi for me, please?
　　請你幫我叫部計程車好嗎？

例 Can you direct me how to go to the museum?
　　可以告訴我怎麼去博物館嗎？

例 Do you know where is the post office?
　　你知道郵局在哪裡嗎？

Chapter 4

飲食

English Travel around the World

已事先訂位 **MP3 067**

I made a reservation at six.

我訂了六點鐘的位子。

實用會話 --

A：Good evening. Two for dinner?
　　晚安！兩人用晚餐嗎？

B：Yes, that's right.
　　是的，沒錯！

A：Did you have a reservation?
　　你有訂位了嗎？

B：Yes, I made a reservation at six.
　　有的，我訂了六點鐘的位子。

同義例句 --

例 I made a reservation yesterday.
　　我昨天有訂位。

例 We had a reservation.
　　我們已經有訂位了。

例 My reservation code is F412.
　　我的預約代號是 F412.

現場訂位

I want a table for 6, please.
我要六個人的位子。

A：Welcome to Four Seasons Restaurant.
歡迎光臨四季餐廳。

B：I want a table for 6, please.
我要六個人的位子。

A：Where would you like to sit?
各位要坐在哪裡？

B：Where would you like to sit, guys?
各位，你們要坐在哪裡？

C：By the window.
要靠窗戶！

同義例句 --

例 I want to make a reservation for 6 people.
我想訂六個人的位子。

說明用餐的人數

For 6.
六個人。

實用會話 --

A：For how many, please?
你要訂幾人(的位子)？

B：For 6.
　　六個人。

A：OK. You may leave your coats here.
　　好的！各位可以把外套放在這裡！

同義例句 --------------------------------

例 There are 6 of us.
　　我們有六個人。

例 We are a group of 6.
　　我們有六個人。

例 A table for 6, please.
　　請給我六個人的位子。

相關例句 --------------------------------

例 I am alone.
　　我一個人。

詢問餐廳是否客滿

Do you have a table available?

現在還有空位嗎？

實用會話 --------------------------------

A：May I help you?
　　需要我幫忙嗎？

B：Do you have a table available?
　　現在還有空位嗎？

A：For how many, sir?
先生，多少人？

B：There are four of us.
我們有四個人。

A：Wait a moment, sir.
請稍等，先生。

同義例句 --

例 Can we have a table?
有空位給我們嗎？

餐廳已經客滿 069

We are quite full tonight.

今晚都客滿了。

實用會話 --

A：Do you have a table available?
現在還有空位嗎？

B：I'm sorry, but we are quite full tonight.
很抱歉，今晚都客滿了。

同義例句 --

例 It's booked up tonight.
今晚都客滿了。

例 I'm afraid all our tables are taken.
恐怕我們所有的位子都坐滿了。

例 I'm afraid we are fully booked for tonight.
今晚的座位恐怕已訂滿了。

例 There are no tables now.
現在沒有座位。

詢問是否願意等空位

Would you mind waiting for 30 minutes?

你介不介意等三十分鐘？

實用會話 --

A：How long do we have to wait?
我們要等多久？

B：Would you mind waiting for 30 minutes?
你介不介意等三十分鐘？

A：No, not at all.
不會，沒關係！

B：Would you mind sitting separately?
各位介不介意分開坐？

A：No, we don't mind.
不會，我們不介意。

同義例句 --

例 I'm afraid you have to wait for 40 minutes.
你恐怕要等四十分鐘。

例 Would you mind waiting until then?
你介意等到那時候嗎？

例 Would you mind waiting until one is free?
你介意等到有空位嗎？

例 Would you mind sharing a table?
你介不介意和其他人併桌？

等待座位安排 070

We can wait.
我們可以等。

A：Welcome. Four for lunch?
歡迎光臨！四位吃午餐嗎？

B：Yes, that's right.
是的，沒錯！

A：You have to wait for about 20 minutes for the non-smoking area. Is it OK?
要非吸煙區的話，你們大概要等廿分鐘。可以嗎？

B：That's all right. We can wait.
沒關係。我們可以等。

同義例句--

例 It's too late.
太晚了！

服務生帶位

This way, please.

這邊請。

實用會話 --

A：We have a table for you now.
我們現在有座位給你了。

B：Thanks.
謝謝！

A：This way, please. Would you like this table by the window?
這邊請。要坐在靠窗戶的座位嗎？

B：Yes, that's nice.
好！這個不錯！

相關例句 ---

例 Watch your step.
請小心腳步。

例 I'm sorry to have kept you waiting.
抱歉讓你久等了。

例 We're very sorry for the delay.
非常抱歉耽擱你的時間。

服務生帶到座位上

How about this table?

這個座位如何？

(實)(用)(會)(話) --

A：How about this table, sir? The view here is great.
先生，這個座位如何？這裡的景觀很棒。

B：OK. We like it.
好的。我們喜歡。

(相)(關)(例)(句) --

例 What do you think of this seat, sir?
先生，你覺得這個座位如何？

例 How do you like it, sir?
先生，你喜歡這個座位嗎？

例 Is this fine with you?
這個(座位)好嗎？

對座位有意見

I don't like this area.

我不喜歡這區。

(實)(用)(會)(話) --

A：This way, please. Watch your step.
這邊請！小心走！

B：Thanks.
謝謝！

A：How do you like this table?
這個位子可以嗎？

B：Well, I don't like this area. Can we have a clean area?
嗯，我不喜歡這區。可以給我們乾淨一點的區域嗎？

A：I'll see what I can do.
我來想辦法！

同義例句 ---

例 Not close to the gate.
不要離門口太近。

例 By the window, if you have.
如果有的話，(給我)靠窗戶的座位。

例 Just not close to the aisle.
只要不要靠近走道。

例 I'd like the seats far away from the rest room.
我想要座位離盥洗室遠一點。

指定座位區域　　　　　　　　　072

We'd like the seats near the window.

我們想要靠窗的座位。

實用會話 ---

A：Please be seated.
請坐。

B：But we'd like the seats near the window.
但是我們想要靠窗戶的座位。

A：How about that seat at the corner?
角落的那個座位可以嗎？

⬤同義例句⬤--

例 We'd like a table by the window.
我們要靠窗戶的位子。

例 But I'd like a table on the side.
但是我想要靠邊的座位。

例 But I don't like this seat.
但是我不喜歡這個座位。

自行指定座位

Could we take these two seats?
我們可以要這兩個座位嗎？

⬤實用會話⬤--

A：Excuse me, could we take these two seats?
抱歉，我們可以要這兩個座位嗎？

B：Sure. Please be seated.
當然可以。請坐。

⬤同義例句⬤--

例 May I take this seat?
我可以坐這個座位嗎？

例 May we have those two seats?
我們可以坐那兩個座位嗎？

例 Can we have a quieter table?
我們可以選安靜一點的座位嗎？

無法安排指定座位　 MP3 073

We don't have other seats available.

我們沒有其他空位了。

A：We would like the seats near the window.
　　我們想要靠窗戶的座位。

B：I'm sorry, but we don't have other seats available.
　　很抱歉，但是我們沒有其他空位了。

A：OK. Oh, can we have the non-smoking area?
　　好。喔，我們可以坐在非吸煙區嗎？

B：No problem, sir.
　　沒問題的，先生。

同義例句 --

例 I'm afraid that table is reserved.
　　那一桌恐怕有人訂了。

入座後提供開水

Would you please bring me a glass of water?

能幫我送一杯水來嗎？

A：Please be seated, ladies and gentlemen.
　　請坐，各位先生女士。

B：Would you please bring me a glass of water first?
能先幫我送一杯水來嗎？

A：No problem, sir.
沒問題的，先生。

B：Thanks. And could we see the menu?
謝謝！還有，能給我們看菜單嗎？

A：Sure. Wait a moment, please.
好的！請稍等！

同義例句 --

例 May I have a glass of water?
我可以要一杯水嗎？

服務生隨後來服務點餐 MP3 074

I'll be right back for your order.

我待會馬上回來為你服務點餐。

實用會話 --

A：Take your time. I'll be right back for your order.
慢慢來。我待會馬上回來為你服務點餐。

B：Thank you.
謝謝你。

同義例句 --

例 I'll be right back with you.
我待會再來。

相關例句 --

例 A waiter will come to take your order.
會有服務生來服務各位點餐。

看菜單

We'll let you know if we are ready to order.

假使我們準備好要點餐，會讓你知道。

實用會話 --

A：May I see the menu, please?
請給我看菜單。

B：Sure. Here is your menu.
好的！這是你們的菜單。

A：Thank you. We'll let you know if we are ready to order.
謝謝你。假使我們準備好要點餐，會讓你知道。

B：No problem. Take your time.
沒問題。慢慢來。

同義例句 --

例 We are not ready to order now.
我們現在還沒有要點餐。

相關例句 --

例 Can we order later?
我們可以等一下再點餐嗎？

詢問是否要開始點餐　075

May I take your order now?

現在要點餐了嗎？

A：May I take your order now?
　　現在要點餐了嗎？

B：Yes, I'd like a turkey sandwich.
　　是的，我要一個火雞三明治。

A：OK. How about you, sir?
　　好的，先生，你呢？

C：What is that?
　　那是什麼？

A：It's Buffalo Wings.
　　是辣雞翅。

C：It looks delicious. I'll order the same thing.
　　看起來好好吃喔！我要點一樣的。

例 Are you ready to order?
　　準備好點餐了嗎？

尚未決定餐點

We've not decided yet.

我們還沒有決定好。

 實用會話 --

A：Are you ready to order?
　　你們準備好點餐了嗎？

B：Sorry, we've not decided yet.
　　對不起，我們還沒有決定好。

C：Could you give us a few minutes?
　　可以給我們幾分鐘看菜單嗎？

A：Sure, please take your time.
　　好的！請慢慢看！

C：Thanks.
　　謝謝！

同義例句 --

例 I haven't decided yet.
　　我還沒有決定好。

例 We'll order in a few minutes.
　　我們等一下點餐！

沙拉的選擇

What salads do you have?

你們有什麼沙拉？

實用會話 ---

A：What do you want for salad?
　　你要什麼沙拉？

B：What salads do you have?
　　你們有什麼沙拉？

A：We have Mixed Salad, Seafood Salad and Chef's Choice Salad.
　　我們有綜合沙拉、海鮮沙拉和主廚沙拉。

B：I'd like the vegetable salad.
　　我要蔬菜沙拉。

A：Which kind of salad dressing would you prefer?
　　請問要哪一種沙拉佐料？

B：I'd like Thousand Island.
　　我要千島醬。

餐廳的特餐／招牌菜

What is today's special?

今天的特餐是什麼？

實用會話 ---

A：What is today's special?
　　今天的特餐是什麼？

B：It's Fillet Steak.
是菲力牛排。

A：OK. I'd like to order Fillet Steak.
好！我點菲力牛排。

B：OK. Fillet Steak. How about you, madam?
好的！菲力牛排。女士，妳呢？

C：What do you recommend?
你有什麼建議嗎？

B：How about the Roast Chicken? It's the specialty of the house.
要不要試試烤雞？這是本店的招牌！

C：OK. I'll try the Roast Chicken.
好！我要試試烤雞。

同義例句 --

例 What's today's special of the house?
今天餐廳的特餐是什麼？

例 What's the specialty?
招牌菜是什麼？

例 What's the specialty of the restaurant?
餐廳的招牌菜是什麼？

點服務生介紹的餐點

I'll have salmon.

我要點鮭魚。

 -

A：You should try our seafood.
你應該要試試我們的海鮮。

B：It sounds good. I'll have salmon and Sirloin Steak for the lady.
聽起來不錯。我要點鮭魚，女士點沙朗牛排。

A：What would you like with the Sirloin Steak? Maybe some vegetables?
沙朗牛排要選什麼搭配？要不要來一些蔬菜？

B：Yes. Some carrots and some boiled potatoes.
好啊！一些紅蘿蔔還有水煮馬鈴薯。

同義例句 -

例 I'll try it.
我要試這一種。

例 I'll try this one.
我點這一個。

餐點售完／無供應

We don't have Sirloin Steak now.
我們現在沒有沙朗牛排。

實用會話 --

A：May I take your order now?
　　你現在要點餐了嗎？

B：Yes, I'd like to order Sirloin Steak.
　　好的，我要點沙朗牛排。

A：I'm sorry, but we don't have Sirloin Steak now.
　　很抱歉，但是我們現在沒有沙朗牛排。

同義例句 --

例 Sirloin Steak is only available on weekends.
　　沙朗牛排只有在週末供應。

例 Sirloin Steak is sold out.
　　沙朗牛排賣完了。

例 It's been sold out.
　　這(道餐點)已經賣完了。

例 It's not on the menu.
　　菜單上沒有這道菜。

主餐的選擇

I'd like to order Sirloin Steak.

我要點沙朗牛排。

A：Are you ready to order now?
準備好現在要點餐了嗎？

B：Yes, we're ready.
是的，我們準備好了。

A：What do you want for the entrée?
你的正餐要點什麼？

B：I'd like to order Sirloin Steak.
我要點沙朗牛排。

A：How about your order, madam?
女士，妳要點什麼呢？

C：I'll try Roast Chicken.
我要試試烤雞。

同義例句 --

例 I want to order New York steak.
我要點紐約牛排。

例 I'll take the "C" course.
我要點 C 餐。

點相同餐點

Can I have the same as that?

我能點和那個一樣的嗎？

實用會話 --

A：May I take your order now?
我可以幫你點餐了嗎？

B：Both of us would like Fillet Steak.
我們兩個都要菲力牛排。

A：Two Fillet Steaks. How about your order, sir?
兩客菲力牛排。先士，你要點什麼呢？

C：Can I have the same as that?
我能點和那個一樣的嗎？

同義例句 --

例 Same here.
我也是點相同的餐點。

例 I'm going to order the same thing.
我要點一樣的餐。

例 I'll have that, too.
我也要那個。

例 We'd like this course for two, please.
這道菜請給我們來兩人份的。

牛排的熟度 **MP3** 079

Well done, please.

請給我全熟。

A：How would you like your steak cooked?
你的牛排要幾分熟？

B：Well done, please.
請給我全熟。

A：And would you like to order some wine with your meal?
那你想不想點酒搭配你的餐點？

B：No, thanks.
不用，謝謝！

相關例句---

例 Medium, please.
請給我五分熟。

例 Medium rare, please.
請給我四分熟。

例 Rare, please.
請給我三分熟。

例 I'd like to have my steak medium.
我要我的牛排五分熟。

共同食用

I'll have this course for 3 of us.

我要點這道餐給我們三個人。

實用會話 ---

A：Are you ready to order?
　　準備好點餐了嗎？

B：Yes, I'll have this course for 3 of us.
　　是的，我要點這道餐給我們三個人。

A：I think this course will be suitable for two persons.
　　我覺得這道餐點兩個人食用比較適合。

湯點的選擇　 080

I want to try seafood soup.

我要試一試海鮮湯。

實用會話 ---

A：What would you like for the soup?
　　湯點要點什麼呢？

B：What do you have?
　　你們有什麼？

A：We have both clear soup and thick soup.
　　我們清湯和濃湯都有。

B：OK! I want to try seafood soup.
　　好，我要試一試海鮮湯。

A：How about you, madam?
　　女士，妳呢？

C：Onion soup, please.
　　請給我洋蔥湯。

甜點的選擇

I want to try pudding.

我要試試布丁。

實用會話 -

A：How about the dessert?
　　點心呢？

B：I want to try pudding.
　　我要試試布丁。

A：Which flavor would you prefer, walnut or vanilla?
　　你喜歡哪一種口味的，核桃還是香草？

B：The vanilla, please.
　　我要香草的，謝謝！

相關例句 -

例 I want to have chocolate cake.
　　我要點巧克力蛋糕。

例 I'll try ice cream.
　　我要點冰淇淋。

例 I'd like cheese cake.
　　我要點起司蛋糕。

例 I want some cookies, please.
　　我要一些餅乾。

飲料的選擇　　　　　　　　　　　　　　　　　MP3 081

I want something cold.

我想要喝點冷飲。

實用會話

A：Would you like something to drink?
　　要不要來點飲料？

B：Sure. I want something cold.
　　好啊！我想要喝點冷飲。

A：Which would you prefer, tea or coffee?
　　要茶還是咖啡？

B：I'd like to have tea.
　　我想喝茶！

A：Would you like to have a cup of rose tea? It's very popular.
　　喝杯玫瑰茶怎麼樣？這個很受歡迎。

B：It sounds terrific. I'll take it.
　　聽起來很棒。我就點這個。

相關例句

例 Coffee would be fine.
　　就點咖啡。

例 Coke, please.
　　請給我可樂。

稍後再繼續點餐

Can we order that later?

我們能等一下再點嗎？

實用會話 ---

A：And a salad?
　要點沙拉嗎？

B：Yes. Bring me a mixed salad with the entrée, please.
　要！請給我綜合沙拉搭配主餐。

A：All right. Will you want dessert?
　好的！要點甜點嗎？

B：Can we order that later?
　我們能等一下再點嗎？

A：Of course.
　當然可以！

完成點餐

That's all for us.

我們就點這些。

實用會話 ---

A：Both of us would like Sirloin Steak.
　我們兩個都要沙朗牛排。

B：Two Sirloin Steaks.
　兩份沙朗牛排。

A：That's right.
　　沒錯！

B：Is that all for your order?
　　你點的就這些嗎？

A：That's all for us.
　　我們就點這些。

同義例句 ---

例 That's it.
　　就這些。

例 That's all, thanks.
　　就這樣，謝謝。

是否要點其他餐點

What else are you going to have?

你還要點什麼嗎？

實用會話 ---

A：What else are you going to have?
　　你還要點什麼嗎？

B：I think it's enough now.
　　我想這就夠了。

A：OK. The meal will be served soon.
　　好的。餐點會盡快為你送上。

B：How long will it take?
　　會需要多久的時間？

A：About twenty minutes.
大概需要廿分鐘。

例 Anything else?
還有沒有要其他(餐點)？

例 Will that be all?
就這樣？

例 Is there anything else?
還要不要別的？

要求再提供麵包

Would you bring us some bread?
能再給我們一些麵包嗎？

A：Excuse me.
不好意思！

B：May I help you, madam?
這位女士，需要我幫忙嗎？

A：Would you bring us some bread?
能再給我們一些麵包嗎？

B：Yes, I'll be right back.
好的，我馬上回來。

相關例句

例 Please give me another sandwich.
請再給我另一份三明治。

例 I want some too, please.
我也要一些。

例 May I have some more wine, please?
我能再多要一些酒嗎？

提供餐點的時間

When would you like your coffee?
你什麼時候要上咖啡？

實用會話 --

A：That's all for now.
先這樣！

B：When would you like your coffee? Now or later?
你什麼時候要上咖啡？現在或稍後？

A：Mine is now, but hers is after the meal.
我的現在上，但是她的用完餐後上。

相關例句 --

例 Right now, please.
請現在就給我。

例 Later, please.
請稍後再上。

餐點延遲

Why is my steak taking so long?
為什麼我的牛排要這麼久？

A：Why is my steak taking so long?
為什麼我的牛排要這麼久？

B：Sorry, sir. I'll check your order right now.
抱歉，先生。我馬上確認你的餐點。

同義例句---

例 Could you serve us quickly?
你能不能快一點為我們上菜？

例 I ordered my meal forty minutes ago and it still hasn't come.
我四十分前點的餐點，到現在還沒有來。

侍者送上餐點

Yes, please.
好的，請便。

A：May I serve your meal now?
現在可以上你的餐點嗎？

B：Yes, please.
好的，請便。

A：You ordered the beef sandwich, right?
你點牛肉三明治，對吧？

B：No. That's hers.
不是。那是她(點)的。

A：Sorry, sir. Who has the onion rings?
抱歉，先生。誰點洋蔥圈？

C：They are ours. We are sharing them.
他們是我們（點）的。我們要一起吃。

相關例句 --

例 May I serve your soup now?
我現在可以上你的湯點嗎？

例 Please have them with this sauce.
請沾這個醬料食用。

例 Is this yours?
這是你點的嗎？

例 Your Sirloin Steak, sir.
先生，你的沙朗牛排(要上菜了)。

送錯／少送餐點　　　　　　　　　　 085

This is not what I ordered.

這不是我點的餐點。

實用會話 --

A：You ordered the steak, right?
你點牛排，對嗎？

B：No, this is not what I ordered.
　　不是，這不是我點的餐點。

A：Sorry, sir. I'll check your order right now.
　　抱歉，先生。我馬上查你的餐點。

同義例句 --

例 Is there a dish missing?
　　是不是少送一道餐點？

例 I'm afraid there is a dish missing.
　　恐怕有一道餐點沒來。

例 Where are my onion rings?
　　我的洋蔥圈呢？

相關例句 --

例 I'm very sorry, sir. What was your order?
　　先生，真對不起。你點的是什麼？

例 I'm very sorry for the mistake.
　　抱歉弄錯了！

例 I'll check your order with our Chef.
　　我會和我們主廚核對你點的餐點。

I'll take both kinds of dressing.
兩種牛排醬料我都要。

實用會話 --

A：What would you like for the dressing?
　　你要哪一種醬料？

B：I'll take both kinds of dressing.
兩種醬料我都要。

A：No problem, sir. How about you, madam?
沒問題的，先生。這位女士，妳呢？

C：No, thanks.
我不用，謝謝！

相關例句 -

例 Black pepper, please.
請給我黑胡椒。

咖啡續杯　

May I have a refill?

我可以續杯嗎？

 -

A：Excuse me.
請問一下！

B：Yes. sir. Can I get you anything else?
先生，請說。需要幫你們拿些其他東西嗎？

A：May I have a refill?
我可以續杯嗎？

B：Of course, sir. Do you need anything else?
當然可以，先生。還需要其他東西嗎？

A：No, thanks.
不用了，謝謝！

同義例句 --

例 May I have another cup?
可以再給我一杯嗎?

例 May I have some more coffee?
我能多要一些咖啡嗎?

呼叫服務生

Excuse me.
請問一下!

實用會話 --

A：Excuse me.
請問一下!

B：Yes, sir, may I help you?
是的,先生,需要我幫忙嗎?

A：Could you bring us a few napkins?
可以給我們一些紙巾嗎?

B：No problem, sir. I'll be right back with you.
沒問題的,先生,我馬上回來!

同義例句 --

例 Waiter!
服務生,請過來!(適用在男性服務生)

例 Waitress!
服務生,請過來!(適用在女性服務生)

餐具出狀況　 087

I dropped my spoon on the floor.
我的湯匙掉在地上了。

實用會話 --

A：I dropped my spoon on the floor. May I have a new one?
　　我的湯匙掉在地上了。我能要一支新的嗎？

B：OK. I'll change a new one for you.
　　好的！我會幫你換支新的。

A：Thank you.
　　謝謝！

同義例句 --

例 This spoon is a little dirty.
　　這支湯匙有一點髒。

例 This glass is cracked!
　　這個玻璃杯有裂痕！

例 My plate is chipped!
　　我的盤子有缺口！

整理桌面

Would you clear the table for us?

你可以為我們整理一下桌子嗎？

實用會話 ------

A：Waitress!
服務生，請過來！（適用在女性服務生）

B：Yes, sir?
先生，有什麼事？

A：Would you clear the table for us?
你可以為我們整理一下桌子嗎？

B：Sure. I'll be right back.
好的。我馬上回來。

相關例句 ------

例 May I take your plate now?
我現在可以收走你的盤子了嗎？

是否已經用完餐點　　　　　　　　　　　 088

We have finished it.

我們用完餐了。

實用會話 ------

A：Have you finished or still working on it?
你用完餐或是還要繼續用餐？

B：We have finished it.
我們用完餐了。

A：May I clear your table?
　　需要我幫你清理桌面嗎？

B：Please. Oh, leave that left.
　　麻煩你囉！喔，那個留下來。

同義例句 --

例 I'm still working on it.
　　我還在用餐。

結帳

Bill, please.

請買單。

實用會話 --

A：Bill, please.
　　請買單。

B：Cash or credit card?
　　用現金還是信用卡付帳？

A：Do you accept Visa?
　　你們有收 Visa 卡嗎？

B：Yes, we do, sir.
　　有的，先生！

同義例句 --

例 Check, please.
　　請結帳。

例 Can I have the check, please?
　　請結帳！

付款方式 **MP3** 089

I'll pay it by credit card.
我要用信用卡結帳。

A : Is the service charge included?
　　有包含服務費嗎？

B : Yes. It's included 10 % service charge.
　　有的。包含百分之十的服務費。

A : OK!
　　好的！

B : Would you pay it by cash or credit cards?
　　你要用現金還是信用卡付帳？

A : I'll pay it by credit card.
　　我要用信用卡結帳。

同義例句 -------------------------------

例 I'll pay it by cash. Here you are.
　　我要用現金付錢。錢在這裡。

例 I'll pay cash.
　　我付現金！

相關例句 -------------------------------

例 Do you take American Express?
　　你們有收美國運通卡嗎？

各自結帳

Let's go Dutch.
讓我們各付各的吧！

A：Bill, please.
　　請給我帳單！

B：Here you are. Would you like to separate your checks?
　　在這裡！各位要分開結帳嗎？

A：I'll treat you.
　　我請你。

C：Come on. Let's go Dutch.
　　好了，讓我們各付各的吧！

A：Good idea.
　　好主意。

例 We'd like to pay separately.
　　我們要分開結帳！

例 Let's split the bill.
　　我們分攤費用吧！

(相)(關)(例)(句) --------------------------------------

例 I insist on paying the bill.
　　我來付帳！

速食店點餐 MP3 090

Give me a chicken hamburger, please.

我要點雞肉漢堡。

實用會話 ---

A：Will that be for here or to go?
要內用還是外帶？

B：To go, please.
外帶，謝謝。

A：What can I get for you?
你要點什麼呢？

B：Give me a chicken hamburger, please. And no on-
ions, please.
我要點雞肉漢堡。不要放洋蔥，謝謝！

A：OK. How about something to drink?
好的！要不要點飲料？

B：A Coke, please.
一杯可樂，謝謝！

A：OK, sir, wait a moment, please.
好的，請稍等。

相關例句 ---

例 I'd like a hamburger with lettuce and tomato.
我要點漢堡，要加生菜和蕃茄。

例 I'll have a piece of apple pie.
我要一片蘋果派。

Chapter 5

交通・觀光

English Travel around the World

搭計程車

Where can I take a taxi?

我可以在哪裡招到計程車？

A：Where can I take a taxi?
　　我可以在哪裡招到計程車？

B：The taxi station is right on the corner.
　　計程車招呼站就在街角。

A：Thanks.
　　謝謝！

同義例句 --------------------------------------

例 Could you call me a cab?
　　可以幫我叫計程車嗎？

相關例句 --------------------------------------

例 Taxi!
　　計程車！(招呼計程車時使用)

告訴司機目的地

City Hall, please.

請到市政府。

A：Taxi!
　　計程車！

B：Where to?
你要去哪裡？

A：City Hall, please.
請到市政府。

B：No problem, sir.
沒問題的，先生。

同義例句 -------------------------------------

例 Can you get me out there?
你能不能載我去那邊？

例 Please take me to this address.
請載我到這個地址。

例 Please to this place.
請到這個地方。（拿出地圖或紙條）

盡速抵達 MP3 092

Could you drive faster?

你能開快一點嗎？

 實用會話 ------------------------------------

A：What time is it now?
現在幾點鐘？

B：It's ten thirty, sir.
現在十點半，先生。

A：Could you drive faster?
你能開快一點嗎？

B：Yes, sir.
　　是的，先生。

A：I have to be there by 11 o'clock.
　　我要在十一點鐘前到那裡。

B：Don't worry about it, sir. You'll be there on time.
　　先生，不用擔心！你會準時抵達的！

相關例句 --

例 Hey, slow down. I'm not in a hurry.
　　嘿，開慢一點！我不趕時間。

抵達目的地下車

Let me off at the traffic light.

讓我在紅綠燈處下車。

實用會話 --

A：Let me off at the traffic light.
　　讓我在紅綠燈處下車。

B：Yes, sir. Here you are.
　　好的，先生。到了。

A：Is this the Buffalo station?
　　這是水牛城車站嗎？

B：Yes, it is.
　　是的。

同義例句 --

例 Let me off at the third building.
　　讓我在第三棟大樓(前)下車。

例 Just drop me off at the next corner.
下一個轉彎讓我下車就行了。

計程車車資

How much is the fare?
車資是多少？

A：Here you are.
到了。

B：How much is the fare?
車資是多少？

A：Two hundred and fifty dollars.
二百五十元。

B：Here you are. Keep the change.
給你！不用找零了！

A：Thank you, sir.
謝謝你，先生。

例 How much?
多少錢？

搭公車的站數

How many stops are there to Buffalo?

到水牛城有多少站？

A：How many stops are there to Buffalo?
　　到水牛城有多少個站？

B：That's the sixth stop.
　　那是第六個站。

A：Where is the bus station?
　　公車總站在哪裡？

B：Go straight ahead about four blocks, and you will
　　see it.
　　直走四個街區，你就會看到。

同義例句 ---

例 How many stops is it to Buffalo?
　　到水牛城要幾站？

搭哪一班公車

Which bus could I get on to Times Square?

我應該搭哪一班公車去時代廣場？

A：Which bus could I get on to Times Square?
　　我應該搭哪一班公車去時代廣場？

B：You can take the 847 or the 105.
　　你可以搭847號或105(公車)。

A：Where is the bus station?
　　公車站在哪裡？

B：Turn right and you'll see the bus station.
　　在轉你就會看到公車站。

A：Thank you so much.
　　非常感謝！

 同義例句 -

例 Which way should I get on the bus?
　　我應該走哪條路去搭公車？

公車的目的地

Does this bus go to City Hall?

這班公車有到市府嗎？

實用會話 -

A：Does this bus go to City Hall?
　　這班公車有到市府嗎？

B：Yes, it goes to City Hall.
　　有的，有到市府。

 同義例句 -

例 Does this bus stop at City Hall?
　　這班公車有停在市政府嗎？

相關例句 --

例 Is this bus stop for City Hall?
這個站牌有(車)到市政府嗎？

例 Does this bus go to the railway station?
這班公車有到火車站嗎？

例 Is this the right bus to the railway station?
這是去火車站的公車嗎？

例 It only goes as far as the railway station.
這班公車只到火車站。

發車的頻率　　　　　　　　　　　　 095

How often does this bus run?
公車多久來一班？

實用會話 --

A：Excuse me?
請問一下！

B：Yes?
請說。

A：How often does this bus run?
公車多久來一班？

B：About 20 minutes.
大約廿分鐘。

A：I see. Thank you. Let's go, honey.
我知道了！謝謝！親愛的，我們走吧！

C：OK.
好！

發車的時間

When will the bus depart?

公車什麼時候開？

A：When will the bus depart?
　　公車什麼時候開？

B：It starts out at 10 am.
　　早上十點鐘就開車了。

A：What time is it now?
　　現在幾點鐘？

B：It's five to ten.
　　還有五分就十點了。

A：Oh, thanks. I gotta go now.
　　喔，謝謝！我現在就要走囉！

例 What time is the next bus for Buffalo?
　　下一班到水牛城的公車是什麼時候？

搭公車的時程　　　　　　　　　　　　　

How long is the ride?

這一趟車程要多久？

A：Excuse me. How long is the ride?
　　請問一下，這一趟車程要多久？

B：It will take about 45 minutes.
　　大要需要四十五分鐘。

A：45 minutes?
　　要四十五分鐘？

C：Are we gonna be late?
　　我們會遲到嗎？

A：I'm afraid so.
　　可能喔！

同義例句 --

例 Is this a long ride?
　　車程要很長的時間嗎？

例 How long does it take to get there?
　　到那裡要多久的時間？

例 How long does this bus trip take?
　　坐公車要多久的時間？

預估到站時間

When will I reach Buffalo?
我什麼時候可以到水牛城？

 實用會話 --

A：Which stop should I get off at?
　　我應該在哪一站下車？

B：You can get off at the Buffalo Hospital.
　　你應該在水牛城醫院下車。

A：When will I reach Buffalo?
我什麼時候可以到水牛城？

B：About 7 pm.
大概晚上七點鐘。

 相關例句 --

例 Where should I get off?
我要在哪裡下車？

例 Where should I get off to go to Buffalo?
到水牛城我要在哪裡下車？

何處買公車票

 MP3 097

Where can I buy the tickets?
哪裡可以買車票？

實用會話 --

A：Where can I buy the tickets?
哪裡可以買車票？

B：It's on the corner.
就在那個角落。

A：Thanks a lot.
多謝啦！

B：No problem.
不客氣！

A：An adult to Buffalo, please.
一張成人票到水牛城，謝謝！

C：$5.

五元！

A：Here you are.

錢給你！

同義例句 --

例 Where can I buy a ticket to Buffalo?

哪裡可以買到水牛城的車票？

買公車票

I'd like to buy a ticket to Buffalo, please.

我要買一張到水牛城的車票。

實用會話 --

A：I'd like to buy a ticket to Buffalo, please.

我要買一張到水牛城的車票。

B：$10.

十元。

A：Here you are.

給你！

相關例句 --

例 A one-way ticket to Buffalo, please.

一張到水牛城的單程車票。

例 A round-trip ticket to Buffalo, please.

一張到水牛城的來回票。

例 To Buffalo for one adult and one child, please.
請給我一張大人、一張小孩到水牛城的票。

例 Two tickets to Buffalo, adult.
兩張到水牛城的票，要成人票。

公車上投錢   098

Exact change only.
只收零錢！

實用會話 --

A：Does this bus go to 15th Street?
這班公車有到第十五街嗎？

B：Yes it does.
有的！

A：What's the fare?
多少錢？

B：75 cents.
七十五分。

A：OK. Here is a dollar.
好，這是一塊錢！

B：Can't you read? "Exact change only."
你不認識字嗎？只收零錢！

A：Oh, OK. I have three quarters here.
喔，好吧！我這裡有三個45分。

請求告知到站

Would you please tell me when we get there?

我們到達時可否告訴我一聲？

A：Honey, where are we now?
親愛的，我們現在在哪裡？

B：I don't really know.
我不太知道耶！

C：May I help you?
需要我的協助嗎？

B：Yes. We're going to Buffalo. Would you please tell me when we get there?
是的。我們要去水牛城。我們到達時可否告訴我一聲？

C：Of course.
當然好。

同義例句 --

例 Please tell me when to get off.
請告訴我何時要下車。

搭公車要求下車

Let me off here, please.

我要在這裡下車。

A：Here you are.
　　我們到了！

B：Is this the Four Seasons Hotel?
　　這是四季飯店嗎？

A：Yes, it is.
　　是的！

B：Let me off here, please.
　　我要在這裡下車。

A：Sure.
　　好的。

相關例句--

例 I missed my stop.
　　我錯過下車站牌了！

搭火車

Which line should I take for Buffalo?

我應該搭哪一線去水牛城？

A：Which line should I take for Buffalo?
　　我應該搭哪一線去水牛城？

B：You can check the subway map over there.
　　你可以查在那裡的地鐵圖。

 同義例句 --------------------------------

例 Which train can I take to Buffalo?
　　我要去水牛城應該搭哪一列車？

例 Which train goes to Buffalo?
　　哪一班車到水牛城？

 相關例句 --------------------------------

例 Where should I get on the train?
　　我應該到哪裡搭火車？

例 How do I get on the train?
　　我要如何搭火車？

搭車月台　　　　　　　　　　 100

Which platform is it on?

在哪一個月台？

實用會話 --------------------------------

A：Is this the right line for Buffalo?
　　去水牛城是這條路線嗎？

B：Yes.
　　是的！

A：Which platform is it on?
　　在哪一個月台？

B：It's on the 2nd platform.
在第二月台。

A：I see. Thank you.
我知道了！謝謝！

(同)(義)(例)(句)--

例 Is this the right platform for Buffalo?
這是出發到水牛城的月台嗎？

(相)(關)(例)(句)--

例 Is this the right train for downtown?
這是去市中心的火車嗎？

何處轉車

Where should I transfer to Buffalo?
我要到哪裡轉車到水牛城？

(實)(用)(會)(話)--

A：Where should I transfer to Buffalo?
我要到哪裡轉車到水牛城？

B：When you arrive at the First Station, you get off and change the red line for Buffalo.
當你到達第一車站後下車，轉搭紅線到水牛城。

(同)(義)(例)(句)--

例 Where should I change trains for Buffalo?
去水牛城要去哪裡換車？

例 What train should I change to?
我要換哪一班列車？

租車費用　　　　　　　　　　　　　　MP3 101

What's the rate for a car?

租一輛車要多少錢？

實用會話 --------------------------------------

A：I'd like some information about renting a car.
我要知道一些租車的資訊。

B：What do you want to know?
你想要知道什麼？

A：What's the rate for a car?
租一輛車要多少錢？

B：The daily rate is 1,500 dollars.
每天的租金是一千五百元。

A：Does this price include insurance?
這個價格有包含保險嗎？

同義例句 --------------------------------------

例 How much is it to rent a car?
租一輛車要多少錢？

例 How much does it cost to rent a car?
租一輛車需要多少錢？

相關例句 --------------------------------------

例 What does this insurance cover?
這個保險包括哪些？

租特定廠牌車輛的費用

What's the weekly rate for a Toyota?

租一輛豐田的車一星期要多少錢？

實用會話 --

A：What's the weekly rate for a Toyota?
　　租一輛豐田的車一星期要多少錢？

B：It's $6,000 a week.
　　一個星期要六千元。

A：6,000? So expensive?
　　六千？要這麼貴喔？

B：Yeah. Do you still want it?
　　是啊！你還要嗎？

同義例句 --

例 If I want to rent a van, how much would it cost?
　　如果我想租一輛休旅車，要多少錢？

預約租車　　　　　　　　　　　　　　　　　　 102

I'd like to rent a car.

我要租車。

A：I'd like to rent a car.
　　我要租車。

B：Did you have a reservation?
　　你有預約了嗎？

A：Yes, my name is Simon.

有，我的名字是賽門。

B：Your driver's license, please.

請給我你的駕照。

A：Sure, here you are.

好，在這裡！

同義例句 --

例 I'd like to reserve a wagon.

我要預約一輛休旅車。

例 I'd like to reserve a Toyota for a week.

我要預約一個星期的豐田的車。

領車

I'd like a Buick.

我要別克的車。

實用會話 ---

A：I'd like to rent a car.

我要租一輛車。

B：Did you have a reservation?

你有預約了嗎？

A：Yes. My name is David Jones.

有的！我的名字是大衛・瓊斯。

B：OK! Which car would you like?

好的！你要哪一種車？

A：I'd like a Buick.
我要別克的車。

明天就要用車 103

Could I have one for tomorrow morning?

我明天早上就能用車嗎？

A：I'd like to rent a car.
我要租車。

B：OK. Fill in this form.
好的，填寫這張表格吧！

A：Could I have one for tomorrow morning?
我明天早上就能用車嗎？

B：Yes. Do you have your driver's license?
可以！你有帶駕照嗎？

A：Sure, here it is.
好，這裡！

同義例句

例 I'll take it right now, if possible.
如果可以的話，我現在就要(用車)。

租車的時間

I'll need it from this Monday to Friday.

我這個星期一到星期五會需要這輛車。

實用會話 --

A：When do you want the car?

你什麼時候要用車？

B：I'll need it from this Monday to Friday.

我這個星期一到星期五會需要這輛車。

A：The daily rate is $1,500.

每天的租金是一千五百元。

同義例句 --

例 I'd like to rent this car for a week.

我要租這輛車一個星期的時間。

租車時填寫資料

MP3 104

Complete this form and sign your name at the bottom.

填寫這份表格，然後在最下面簽上你的姓名。

實用會話 --

A：I'll need it from this Monday to Friday.

我這個星期一到星期五要(租)這部車。

B：May I see your driver's license?

可以給我看你的駕照嗎？

A：Yes, it's right here.
好，在這裡！

B：OK. Now complete this form and sign your name at the bottom.
好的。現在請填寫這份表格，然後在最下面簽上你的姓名。

A：Sure.
好！

例 Please fill up this form.
填寫這張表格。

車子的保險

Does this price include full insurance?

這個價格有包含全險嗎？

A：Sure. Here you are.
好的！在這裡。

B：Could you please show me the rate list? Does this price include full insurance?
可以給我看價目表嗎？這個價格有包含全險嗎？

A：Of course.
當然有！

B：OK. I'll rent a Toyota. I want to rent a wagon.
好的，我要租一輛豐田汽車。我要租休旅車。

A：Can I see your driver's license?
我能看你的駕照嗎？

(相)(關)(例)(句)--

例 Let me see your driver's license.
讓我看看你的駕照。

還車的地點

Do I have to return the car here?

我要回到這裡還車嗎？

(實)(用)(會)(話)---

A：How much does it cost to rent a car?
租用一輛車需要多少錢？

B：You will have to use a credit card or leave a $500 deposit.
你需要用信用卡付費或付五百元的保證金。

A：Do I have to return the car here?
我要回到這裡還車嗎？

B：No. You may return it to our branches anywhere.
不必。你可以在我們任何地方的分公司還車。

(相)(關)(例)(句)--

例 Can I leave the car at any agency?
我可以在其他車行還車嗎？

索取市區地圖

May I have a map of this city?

我可以要一張市區地圖嗎？

實用會話 --

A：May I have a map of this city?
　我可以要一張市區地圖嗎？

B：Yes. Here you are.
　好的。給你。

A：Do you have brochures about the Phantom of the Opera?
　你有「歌劇魅影」的手冊嗎？

B：Of course. Here you are.
　當然有！給你！

同義例句 --

例 Is there a free city map?
　有免費的城市地圖嗎？

例 Do you have any maps of the downtown?
　你們有市中心的地圖嗎？

例 Do you have any tour brochures?
　你們有旅遊手冊嗎？

索取訊息簡介　　　　　　　　　　　　MP3 106

Which one has information about Cats?

哪一個有關於「貓劇」的訊息？

實用會話 --------------------------------

A：May I have some brochures for the city tours?
　　可以給我一些市區旅遊的簡介嗎？

B：Sure, here you are.
　　好，給你！

A：Which one has information about Cats?
　　哪一個有關於「貓劇」的訊息？

B：You probably need those brochures.
　　你可能需要那些簡介。

同義例句 --------------------------------

例 Do you have a guide for plays?
　　你們有沒有戲劇指南？

例 Where can I get some information about sightseeing tours?
　　哪裡可以得到有關觀光旅遊的訊息？

觀光行程的種類

What kind of tour do you have?
你們有哪一種行程？

實用會話 --

A：What kind of tour do you have?
你們有哪一種行程？

B：How do you like sightseeing buses?
你覺得市區巴士觀光如何？

A：Sightseeing? I don't think so.
觀光？我不想要耶！

B：OK. How about the casino tour?
好吧！要不要參加賭場行程？

A：Terrific. I'd love it. What do you think, sweetie?
太好了！我喜歡！親愛的，你覺得呢？

C：But this is our honey moon trip.
可是這是我們的蜜月旅行啊！

同義例句 --

例 How about the Statue of Liberty?
你覺得自由女神像如何？

詢問是否有當地旅遊團 **MP3 107**

Do you have any good package tours?

你們有不錯的套裝行程嗎?

A：Do you have any good package tours?
　　你們有好的套裝行程嗎?

B：Yes. We can arrange a city tour for you.
　　有的。我們可以幫你安排市區旅遊。

A：How much will it cost?
　　要多少錢?

同義例句 ------------------------------------

例 Do you have any other tours that go to museums?
　　你們有任何去博物館的旅遊行程嗎?

例 Is there any tour for Disneyland?
　　有沒有去迪士尼樂園的旅遊行程?

例 Can you arrange a night bus tour?
　　可以安排夜間的巴士旅遊嗎?

詢問行程安排

Are there any special places I should visit?

有沒有一些特殊的地方我應該去參觀？

實用會話 -

A：Are there any special places I should visit?
有沒有一些特殊的地方我應該去參觀？

B：How about the tour of the Central Park?
你覺得中央公園的行程如何？

A：Well, it's not what I want.
嗯，我不是要這個！

B：OK. How about the three-day sea cruise?
好吧！要不要嘗試三天的海上旅遊？

同義例句 -

例 What tour should I take?
我應該參加哪一種行程？

例 Is that building worth visiting?
那棟大樓值得參觀嗎？

推薦旅遊行程

 MP3 108

What tour do you recommend?

你推薦哪一種行程？

實用會話 --

A：What tour do you recommend?
　　你推薦哪一種行程？

B：How about two-day tour? It includes Disneyland and sea cruise.
　　兩日遊行程如何？包括迪士尼樂園和海上旅遊。

A：I'd love to try.
　　我想試試看。

B：Good. Here is the application form.
　　好！這是申請表格！

同義例句 --

例 What sights do you recommend?
　　你推薦哪一些觀光點？

例 Which tour do you suggest?
　　你建議哪一種旅遊團？

例 Do you have any ideas about good sightseeing places?
　　你知道任何不錯的觀光景點嗎？

相關例句 --

例 I'm interested in this tour.
　　我對這個旅遊行程有興趣。

觀光行經路線

Does this tour include the art gallery?

旅遊行程有包括美術館嗎？

實用會話 -

A：It's only 500 dollars. You can visit the art gallery or the museum.
只要五百元。你可以參觀美術館或博物館。

B：Does this tour include the art gallery?
這趟旅遊行程有包括美術館嗎？

A：No, it just passes by the art gallery.
沒有，只有經過美術館而已。

相關例句 -

例 Will we visit the City Hall?
我們會參觀市府嗎？

例 What does it include in the night tour?
夜間旅遊包含哪些？

例 Does this tour include the Grand Canyon?
這個旅遊行程有包含大峽谷嗎？

例 Does this tour go to the National Park?
這個旅遊行程有去國家公園嗎？

觀光行程花費的時間 MP3 109

How many days does this city tour take?

這個市區行程要多久的時間？

實用會話 --

A：Maybe you're interested in the city tour.
　　你可能對市區旅遊有興趣。

B：How many days does this city tour take?
　　這個市區行程要多久的時間？

A：It'll take 2 days.
　　要兩天的時間。

B：No. I won't stay here for 2 days.
　　沒辦法！我不會停留兩天的時間。

同義例句 --

例 How many hours does it take?
　　要花幾個小時的時間？

例 How long will it be?
　　要多久的時間？

例 What time will it be over?
　　幾點會結束？

旅遊團的預算

What's your budget?

你們的預算是多少？

A：What's your budget?
你們的預算是多少？

B：Not too much. It's about 4 thousand.
不太多。大約四千元。

A：OK. Here is my suggestion. You may join the city tour. It includes the The Metropolitan Museum of Art.
好！這是我的建議。你可以參加城市的觀光行程。有包含美國大都會博物館。

B：It sounds good. OK, I'll take it.
聽起來不錯。好，我要參加。

例 We have to keep budget below 1,000 dollars.
我們需要把預算控制在一千元以下。

旅遊團費用

What's the price of the half day tour?
半天的旅遊行程要多少錢？

A：What's the price of the half-day tour?
　　半天的旅遊行程要多少錢？

B：It's 2,000 dollars for one person.
　　每一個人要兩千元。

A：By the way, I'd like to join the Casino tour.
　　對了，我要參加賭場的行程。

B：OK. Please fill in the application form.
　　好。請填寫申請表格！

相關例句

例 What's the price for that tour?
　　那個旅遊行程多少錢？

例 What's the price of the full-day city tour?
　　市區一日遊的費用是多少？

例 How much will it cost for kids?
　　小孩子要多少錢？

例 What's the price for an adult?
　　大人的費用要多少？

例 How much will it cost for one person?
　　一個人要多少錢？

旅遊團費用明細

Is the tour all-inclusive?

行程包括所有的費用嗎?

實用會話 --

A：I'd like to join this city night tour.
我要參加市區夜間旅遊。

B：OK. Here is the registration form.
好的,這是註冊表格。

A：Is the tour all-inclusive?
行程有包括所有的費用嗎?

B：Yes, the round-trip fare, and the meals are included.
是的,包括來回車資和餐費。

相關例句 --

例 Is there any meals included?
有包含餐點嗎?

例 Does this price include meals?
這個價錢有包含餐點嗎?

例 Is there a pick up service at the hotel?
有沒有到飯店接送的服務呢?

例 Does it include an English speaking guide?
有包括會說英文的導遊嗎?

旅遊團出發的時間

What time does the tour start?

旅遊團幾點開始？

A：Where shall we meet?
　　我們何地何時要集合？

B：In front of the station.
　　在車站前。

A：What time does the tour start?
　　旅遊團幾點開始？

B：The bus meets in front of the hotel at 9 am.
　　巴士早上九點鐘在飯店前集合。

相關例句 --

例 The tour guide will be here to pick you up around
9 o'clock.
導遊會在九點鐘左右來這裡接你。

預約旅遊團

Can I make a reservation here for tomorrow?

我能在這裡預約明天（的行程）嗎？

A：I'm interested in the art gallery tour.
　　我對美術館行程有興趣。

B：OK. Here is the registration form. Please fill it in.
　　好的。這是登記表格,請先填寫。

A：Can I make a reservation here for tomorrow?
　　我能在這裡預約明天的行程嗎?

B：Sure. May I have your name, please?
　　好的。請問你的大名?

相關例句 --

例 Could you reserve this tour for two of us?
　 你能幫我們兩個人預約這個旅遊行程嗎?

例 I'd like to join the full-day city tour.
　 我要參加市區一日遊行程。

例 I'd like to join the city tour.
　 我想要參加市區旅遊。

例 I'd like to join the sea cruise tomorrow.
　 我要參加明天的遊艇行程。

例 I'd rather go on a half-day tour.
　 我比較想參加半天的行程。

旅遊團自由活動的時間 112

How long are we staying here?
我們要在這裡停留多久?

實用會話 --

A：We'll have a thirty-minute break now.
　　我們現在有卅分鐘的休息時間。

B：How long are we staying here?
　　我們要在這裡停留多久?

A：Let's see. About two hours.
　　我看看！大約兩個小時。

B：I see. Thanks. Come on, let's go, honey.
　　我知道了！謝謝！親愛的，來吧，我們走吧！

C：We've got plenty of time to see around.
　　我們有的是時間到處看看。

（同）（義）（例）（句）--

例 When shall we come back here?
　　我們要幾點回這裡來？

（相）（關）（例）（句）--

例 Do we have time to drop in at the art gallery?
　　我們有空進去美術館看看嗎？

例 Do we have time to buy some souvenirs?
　　我們有時間買一些紀念品嗎？

門票

What's the admission fee?

門票是多少？

（實）（用）（會）（話）--

A：What's the admission fee?
　　門票是多少？

B：It's 100 dollars per person.
　　一個人要一百元。

A：What opera is performing tonight?
　　今晚上演哪一部歌劇？

B：It's Cats.
　　是貓劇。

例 Is the admission fee included?
　　門票都是有包括（在費用內）嗎？

開演及結束時間

What time does this show start?

這場秀什麼時候開始？

實用會話 --

A：What time does this show start?
　　這場秀什麼時候開始？

B：At 7 o'clock.
　　在七點鐘（開始）。

A：What time did you say?
　　你說幾點鐘？

B：7 o'clock.
　　七點鐘！

A：Hurry up, honey, we're late for the show.
　　親愛的，快一點，這場表演我們要遲到了！

相關例句 --
例 What time does this show end?
　　這場秀什麼時候結束？

是否可以拍照

Can we take pictures in the museum?

我們可以在博物館裡拍照嗎？

 實用會話 ------------------------------------

A：Can we take pictures in the museum?
　　我們可以在博物館裡拍照嗎？

B：No problem, sir.
　　沒問題的，先生。

A：Thank you. Honey, look here. Say cheese.
　　謝謝！親愛的，看這裡，笑一個！

C：Cheese.
　　好！

相關例句 ------------------------------------

例 Can I take a picture here?
　　我可以在這裡拍照嗎？

例 Can I take a picture for you?
　　我可以幫你拍一張照片嗎？

例 Would you please take a picture for me?
　　可以請你幫我拍一張照片嗎？

例 Could you take a picture for us?
　　可以幫我們拍照嗎？

例 Would you mind taking my picture?
　　你介意幫我拍一張照片嗎？

要求解釋問題

What does that mean?

那是什麼意思？

A：What does that mean?
那是什麼意思？

B：It means a dragon in English.
在英文中是表示龍的意思。

A：A dragon? Sounds interesting.
龍？好有趣喔！

B：Yeap. It's magnificent, isn't it?
是啊！很壯觀，對吧？

同義例句 --

例 How do you call it in English?
英文怎麼說那個東西？

例 Would you please explain it to me?
你能解釋給我聽嗎？

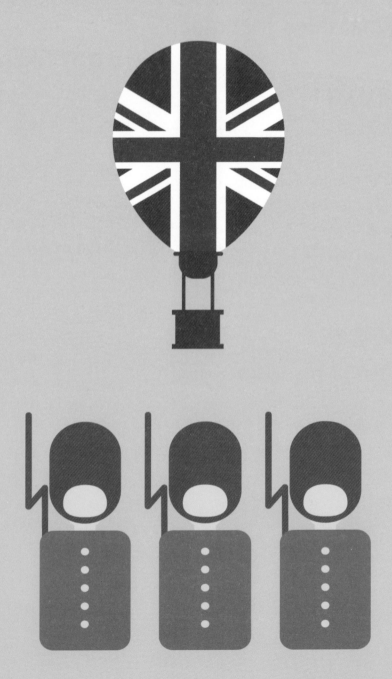

Chapter 6

購物

English Travel around the World

詢問營業時間　　　　　　　　　　　　MP3 115

How late are you open?

你們營業到幾點？

 實用會話 ---

A：How late are you open?
　　你們營業到幾點？

B：We are open until six thirty.
　　我們營業到六點卅分。

相關例句 ---

例 We are open all night.
　　我們整晚都有營業。

例 We are open from 11 am to 9 pm.
　　我們從早上十一點營業到晚上九點鐘。

例 On Saturday we are open from 9 am to 7 pm.
　　星期六我們從早上九點營業到晚上七點鐘。

尋找商品販售區

How should I get to the shoe department?

鞋區在哪裡？

 實用會話 ---

A：Excuse me.
　　請問一下！

B：What can I do for you?
需要我幫忙嗎？

A：How should I get to the shoe department?
鞋區在哪裡？

B：It's on the 2nd floor.
在二樓。

A：Thanks.
謝謝！

相關例句 --

例 In which section can I find the plastic bags?
我可以在哪一區找到塑膠袋？

只看不買 116

I'm just looking around.

我只是隨便看看。

實用會話 --

A：May I help you with something?
需要我幫忙的嗎？

B：No. I'm just looking around.
不用。我只是隨便看看。

A：Let me know if you need anything.
如果有什麼需要，讓我知道一聲。

B：Sure. Thank you.
好的，謝謝你！

同義例句 --

例 No. Thanks.
不用。謝謝！

例 I don't need any help.
我不需要任何服務。

例 Not yet. Thanks.
還不需要。謝謝！

例 Maybe later. Thank you.
也許等一下要（麻煩你），謝謝。

搭配特定商品

I'd like a scarf for my dress.
我想要一條披肩搭配我的洋裝。

實用會話 --

A：What are you looking for?
你在找什麼嗎？

B：I'd like a scarf for my dress.
我想要一條披肩搭配我的洋裝。

A：All right. You might be interested in those new arrivals.
好的！你可能對這些新貨有興趣！

B：Well, I don't like this kind of style.
嗯⋯我不喜歡這種款式。

相關例句 ---

例 Do you carry Mac laptops?
你們有 Mac 的筆電嗎？

例 Do you have any light bulbs for this lamp?
你們有賣適用這個燈的電燈泡嗎？

例 Can I use this plate in an oven?
我可以在烤箱使用這個盤子嗎？

購物的打算　　　　　　　　　　　　　 117

I'm looking for baseball hats.
我在找棒球帽子。

實用會話 ---

A：Is there anything special in mind?
　　心裡有想好要什麼嗎？

B：Yes, I'm looking for baseball hats.
　　有的，我在找棒球帽子。

A：Is it a present for someone?
　　送給誰的禮物嗎？

B：Yes, it's for my boy.
　　是的，是給我兒子的。

A：OK, would you like to take a look at this?
　　好的，你要看一下嗎？

同義例句 ---

例 I need to buy birthday presents for my son.
我需要幫我兒子買生日禮物。

例 I'm looking for some gifts for my kids.
我在找一些要送給孩子們的禮物。

尋找特定的商品

I'm trying to find a Christmas present for my wife.

我想要幫我太太買耶誕節禮物。

 -

A：What do you want to buy?
你想買什麼？

B：I'm trying to find a Christmas present for my wife.
我想要幫我太太買耶誕節禮物。

A：All right. What exactly are you looking for?
好的！你有特定想要找的東西嗎？

B：I'm not sure, really. Maybe you can help me.
我不是很確定！也許你可以幫我！

同義例句 -

例 I need a pair of gloves.
我需要手套。

例 Do you have any purple hats?
你們有紫色的帽子嗎？

購買專輯

Do you have the element of freedom, please?

你們有賣 **the element of freedom** 嗎？

實用會話 --

A：Do you have the element of freedom, please?
你們有賣 the element of freedom 嗎？

B：Who's it by?
誰的？

A：Aleeshia Keys. It's her latest single.
Aleeshia Keys。是她的最新單曲專輯。

B：Let's see... just a minute.
我看看，等一下。

A：Sure.
好！

B：Yes. Here you are.
有，在這裡。

A：Oh, thanks. And do you have the new album by Mary J. Blige?
喔，謝謝！還有，你們有 Mary J. Blige 的新專輯嗎？

B：Stronger with each tear?
是 Stronger with each tear 嗎？

A：Yes.
對！

B：We have that. It's a terrific album. You'll love it.
我們有。這張專輯很棒。你會喜歡的。

A：Oh, it's not for me. It's for my daughter. It's a birthday present.

喔，不是要給我的。是要給我女兒的，是生日禮物。

參觀特定商品 119

May I see those MP3 players?

我能看那些 **MP3** 播放器嗎？

實用會話 --

A：What would you like to see?

你想看些什麼？

B：I'm just looking around.

我只是看一看。

A：Sure. Take your time.

好的，你慢慢看！

B：May I see those MP3 players?

我能看那些 MP3 播放器嗎？

A：Sure. Here you are.

好的，給你！

同義例句 --

例 I'd like to see some ties.

我想看一些領帶。

例 May I have a look at them?

我能看一看它們嗎？

例 Show me that pen.

給我看那支筆。

例 Those skirts look great.
那些裙子看起來不錯。

尋找特定的商品

Please show me that black sweater.
請給我看看那件黑色毛衣。

A：Hello.
嗨！

B：May I help you?
需要我幫忙嗎？

A：Yes, I'm looking for some sweaters.
是的，我在找一些毛衣。

B：Which one do you like?
你喜歡哪一件？

A：Please show me that black sweater.
請給我看看那件黑色毛衣。

同義例句 --

例 I'm looking for a toy for my son.
我要幫我兒子找玩具。

找到中意商品

I'm interested in this one.

我對這個有興趣。

A：Did you find something you like?
　　有找到喜歡的東西了嗎？

B：Not yet. Do you have any hats like this one?
　　還沒有！你們有沒有像這類的帽子？

A：Here you are. Is this what you are looking for?
　　給你！你要找的是這一種嗎？

B：Yes, I'm interested in this one.
　　是的，我對這個有興趣。

同義例句 ------------------------------------

例 It looks nice.
　　這個看起來不錯。

例 Can you show me something different?
　　你能給我看一些不一樣的嗎？

例 I'm interested in this computer.
　　我對這台電腦有興趣。

對商品不滿意

No, I don't like this one.

不要，我不喜歡這一件。

 實用會話 --

A：Do you need a shirt? How about this one?
你需要襯衫嗎？這個怎麼樣？

B：No, I don't like this one.
不要，我不喜歡這一件。

同義例句 --

例 It's not what I need.
這不是我需要的。

例 It's not what I'm looking for.
我不是要找這一種。

相關例句 --

例 Do you have anything better?
你有沒有好一點的？

例 Anything else?
還有其他的嗎？

例 Is that all?
全部就只有這些嗎？

新品上市　 **MP3 121**

They are new arrivals.

他們都是新品。

A：They are new arrivals.
　　他們都是新品。

B：Can I pick it up?
　　我可以拿起來(看看)嗎？

A：Sure.
　　可以！

B：No discount for new arrivals?
　　新品沒有折扣嗎？

A：I'm afraid not, sir.
　　沒辦法，先生。

示範操作

Would you show me how it works?

你可以操作給我看嗎？

A：Would you show me how it works?
　　你可以操作給我看嗎？

B：Sure, sir. You can push this button to turn it on.
　　好的，先生。你可以按這個鈕來開啟電源。

A：How to use this?
這個要怎麼用？

例 How do I operate it?
我要怎麼操作它？

商品保固

Does it have a warranty?

這個有保固期嗎？

A：May I help you?
需要我幫忙嗎？

B：Yes. I'm looking for an iPhone, either the 8GB or 16 GB model.
是的，我要找 iPhone，8GB 或 16GB 的款式。

A：OK. Let me show you this one.
好的！來看這個。

B：Does it have a warranty?
這個有保固期嗎？

A：Yes, it's one-year warranty.
有的，它有一年保固。

例 How long is the warranty on this lamp?
這盞燈的保固期是多久？

例 Do you offer a one-year warranty?
你們有提供一年的保固嗎？

例 Do you offer a life-time warranty?
你們有提供終身的保固嗎？

例 Can I get a warranty on a second-hand notebook?
二手筆記型電腦有保固書嗎？

特定顏色

Do you have this size in any other colors?

有這個尺寸的其他顏色嗎？

實用會話 --

A：Do you have this size in any other colors?
　　有這個尺寸的其他顏色嗎？

B：What color do you like?
　　你想要哪一個顏色？

A：Do you have any ones in blue?
　　你們有藍色的嗎？

B：OK. Let me take some blue skirts for you.
　　好的。讓我拿一些藍色裙子給你。

同義例句 --

例 I'm looking for a pair of blue socks.
我在找藍色的襪子。

例 Both red and blue are OK.
紅色或藍色都可以。

尺寸說明

I don't know my size.

我不知道我的尺寸。

A：I'd like to buy an overcoat for the winter. May I try it on?
我想買冬天穿的大衣。我可以試穿嗎？

B：Sure. What is your size?
可以啊！你的尺寸是多少？

A：I don't know my size.
我不知道我的尺寸。

B：Size 7, I guess.
我猜你要穿七號！

例 My size is between 8 and 7.
我的尺寸是介於八號和七號之間。

例 My size is 8.
我的尺寸是八號。

特定尺寸

I want the large size.

我要大尺寸的。

實用會話

A：Any other sizes?
　　有沒有其他尺寸？

B：This comes in several sizes. What size do you want?
　　這有好多種尺寸。你要什麼尺寸？

A：I want the large size.
　　我要大尺寸的。

B：Let's see... how about size 8?
　　我看看…八號可以嗎？

同義例句

例 I'll try on a small.
　　我要試穿小號的。

例 It's a small and I wear a medium.
　　這是小號的，而我穿中號的。

例 Do you have this one in small?
　　你們有這一種小號的嗎？

例 Give me size 8.
　　給我八號。

例 Size 8 in black.
　　(給我)黑色的八號尺寸。

詢問是否要試穿

Would you like to try it on?

你要試穿看看嗎？

實用會話 --

A：I don't like this color.
我不喜歡這個顏色。

B：Would you like to try it on?
你要試穿看看嗎？

A：No, thanks.
不用了，謝謝。

B：This comes in several colors. How do you like red?
這有好多種顏色。你喜歡紅色嗎？

A：It looks so elegant.
看起來很高雅。

B：Yes, it is.
是啊，的確是！

要求試穿

Can I try this on?

我可以試穿這一件嗎？

實用會話 --

A：Can I try this on?
我可以試穿這一件嗎？

B：Sure. This way, please.
好啊。這邊請。

A：How does this look on me?
我穿這件看起來怎麼樣？

B：Well, it's too short.
嗯，太短了！

A：Really? Let me see the red one, in my size, please.
真的喔？請拿件紅色的給我看看，要合我的尺寸。

B：Sure, just a minute.
好，等一下！

相關例句 --

例 You can try this one.
你可以試穿這一件。

例 Fitting room is over there.
試衣間在那裡。

試穿特定尺寸 125

I should try another bigger one.

我應該要試穿另一件大一點的。

實用會話 --

A：Try this coat on and see if it fits.
試穿這件外套，看看是否合身。

B：I should try another bigger one.
我應該要試穿另一件大一點的。

A：Sure. Here you are.
好的！給你！

B：May I try on that one, too?
我也可以試穿那一件嗎？

A：Sure. How about size 8?
可以！八號可以嗎？

同義例句 --

例 Could I try a larger one?
我可以試穿大一點的嗎？

例 Can I try a smaller one?
我能試穿較小件的嗎？

例 Do you have this color in size 8?
這個顏色有八號嗎？

例 Do you have these shoes in size 7?
你有七號的鞋子嗎？

試穿結果

How does this look on me?
我穿這一件的效果怎麼樣？

實用會話 --

A：Would you like to try on a larger size?
你要試穿大一點尺寸的嗎？

B：Yes, please.
好的，請給我。

A：Here you are.
給你。

B：How does this look on me?
我穿這一件的效果怎麼樣？

A：It looks great on you.
你穿看起來不錯。

B：You think so?
你這麼認為嗎？

相關例句 --

例 Where is the mirror?
鏡子在哪裡？

例 Take a look for me.
幫我看一看。

例 I don't think this is good.
我不覺得這件好。

例 Don't you think it's too loose?
你不覺得太寬鬆嗎？

喜歡試穿結果   126

It feels fine.
我覺得不錯。

實用會話 --

A：Where is the fitting room?
試衣間在哪裡？

B：This way, please.
這邊請！

B：How do they feel?
它們覺得如何？

A：It feels fine. What do you think?
我覺得不錯。你覺得呢？

B：I think it looks perfect to me.
我覺得我穿看起來不錯！

同義例句 --

例 It looks perfect to me.
這個我喜歡。

例 It looks OK on me.
我穿看起來不錯。

例 It's great.
好看。

例 Not bad.
不錯。

特定尺寸不適合

It really feels tight.
真的有一些緊。

實用會話 --

A：Would you like to try on?
你要試穿嗎？

B：Yes, I'll try on size 42.
好的，我要試穿42號。

A：Does it fit?
合身嗎？

B：Well, I don't really know... It really feels tight.
嗯，我不知道耶…，真的有一些緊。

同義例句 ------

例 The legs weren't long enough.
褲腳的長度不夠。

例 They were just too small.
它們太小了。

例 They seem a little big.
好像有一些大。

例 The waist was a little tight.
嗯，腰部有一點緊。

缺貨中

I think we're out of your size.
我想你要的尺寸已經賣完了！

 實用會話 ------

A：Is someone taking care of you?
有人為你服務嗎？

B：No. I'd like a long-sleeved shirt.
沒有！我要長袖的襯衫。

A：How about this one?
這一件怎麼樣？

B：Do you have any in white, size 9?
你們有白色九尺寸的嗎？

A：I think we're out of your size.
我想你要的尺寸已經賣完了！

例 We don't have any left.
我們沒有貨了！

詢問是否會再進貨

Do you think you'll be getting any more in?

你們還會再進貨嗎？

A：Are you being helped?
有人為你服務嗎？

B：No. Do you have brown jackets, size 40?
沒有！你們有賣咖啡色的外套嗎？要四十號。

A：The closest I have is a 38.
我們有的最接近是卅八號。

B：Do you think you'll be getting any more in?
你們還會再進貨嗎？

A：No, but we might have them at our other store.
不會，但是我們的其他倉庫可能有貨。

預訂商品

MP3 128

Can you order one for me?

可以幫我訂一件嗎？

 實用會話 ------------------------------

A：Is anybody waiting on you?
有人為你服務嗎？

B：No. I'm trying to find a green sweater in extra large.
沒有！我要找綠色的大尺寸毛衣。

A：We have your size, but not in that color.
我們有你的尺寸，但是不是那個顏色。

B：Can you order one for me?
可以幫我訂一件嗎？

A：Certainly. Just give me your name and address.
當然可以。請給我你的名字和地址。

要考慮是否喜歡

Let me think about it for a second.

我想一想。

實用會話 ------------------------------

A：Can I try it on?
我可以試穿嗎？

B：Of course. This way, please.
當然可以！這邊請！

A：Thanks.
　　謝謝！

B：How do you like it?
　　你喜歡嗎？

A：Let me think about it for a second.
　　我想一想。

相關例句 --

例 I like this one.
　　我喜歡這一件。

例 I don't like it.
　　我不喜歡。

例 I don't know.
　　我不知道。

其他樣式　　　　　　　　　　　　　　　　MP3 129

This comes in many colors.

這有許多種顏色。

實用會話 --

A：Is that all you have?
　　你們只有這些？

B：No. This comes in many colors.
　　不是的！這有許多種顏色。

A：Any other styles?
　　有沒有其他款式？

B：Sorry, sir, that's all we have.
　　抱歉，先生，這是我們所有的了。

相關例句 --

例 Which brand do you want?
你想要哪一個牌子？

例 What style would you like to see?
你想看什麼款式？

例 How about these ones?
這一些如何？

詢問售價

How much?
多少錢？

實用會話 --

A：It looks perfect to me.
我穿看起來不錯！

B：You know, that sweater's a great buy.
你知道嗎，那件毛衣真的很划算。

A：How much?
多少錢？

B：It's five hundred dollars.
賣五百元。

同義例句 --

例 How much is this?
這個要多少錢。

例 How much does it cost?
這個要賣多少錢？

例 How much did you say?
你說要多少錢？

例 What is the price?
價錢是多少？

含稅價 130

Does this include tax?

這個有含稅嗎？

A：How much did you say?
你說是多少錢？

B：It's $120.
是一百廿元。

A：Does this include tax?
這個有含稅嗎？

B：Yes, it does.
有的，有含稅！

A：OK. I'll take it.
好，我要買！

售價太貴

Can you lower the price?

你可以算便宜一點嗎?

實用會話

A：It costs seven hundred dollars plus tax.
它含稅要七千元。

B：So expensive? I can't afford it.
這麼貴?我付不起。

A：It's worth it.
這個很值得。

B：Can you lower the price a bit if I buy them?
如果我買它們,你可以算便宜一點嗎?

A：I'm afraid not, madam.
抱歉,女士,沒有。

同義例句

例 I can't afford that!
我付不起!

例 I can't pay that much.
我付不起那麼多錢。

例 That's a rip-off!
真是敲竹槓!

例 Your prices are pretty steep.
你們的價格相當高。

例 That much?
太貴了吧?

例 It's too expensive.
太貴了！

例 It's a little expensive.
有一點貴。

討價還價

Are there any discounts?

有沒有折扣？

A：What do you think of the price?
你覺得價格如何？

B：It's too expensive. Are there any discounts?
它太貴了。有沒有折扣？

同義例句 --

例 Can you give me a discount?
你可以給我折扣嗎？

例 Can you make it cheaper?
可以算便宜一點嗎？

例 Do you think it's possible to get a discount?
你認為可以有折扣嗎？

例 Can you lower it two hundred?
可以便宜兩百元嗎？

例 Can you give me a 10 percent discount?
你能給我九折嗎？

例 How about five hundred dollars?
可以算五百元嗎？

例 Can you cut me a deal?
你可以算我便宜一點嗎？

例 Can you come down a little?
可以再便宜一點嗎？

合買 2 件 131

I want both of them.

我兩件都要。

A：Would you like to buy it?
你要買嗎？

B：I want both of them.
我兩件都要。

A：Good. Do you need anything else?
好。還需要其他東西嗎？

B：No, that's all for now.
不用，就這樣！

同義例句 ---

例 I want to buy two of these.
我要買這兩件。

合購議價

Is there a discount for two?

買兩件可以有折扣吧?

實用會話 ---

A:Is there a discount for two?
　　買兩件可以有折扣吧?

B:But you have to pay by cash.
　　可是你要付現金。

A:No problem. How much is it?
　　沒問題!多少錢?

B:I can give you a 10% discount. It's $90.
　　我可以給你九折。要九十元。

A:OK, I'll take it.
　　好,我買!

決定購買

 132

I'll take it.

我要買它。

實用會話 ---

A:Would you show me that toy?
　　可以給我看看那個玩具嗎?

B:Sure. Let me show you how it works.
　　當然可以!我示範給你看怎麼運作的。

A：Wow! It's amazing.
哇！好神奇喔！

B：Would you like to buy it?
你要買嗎？

A：Yes. I'll take it.
要的，我要買它。

同義例句 --

例 I'll buy this one.
我要買這一件。

例 I'll get this one.
我要買這一件。

不打算購買

No, I'll pass this time.

不要，我這次不買。

實用會話 --

A：Does this price include keyboard and mouse?
這個價格有包括鍵盤和滑鼠嗎？

B：No, it doesn't.
沒有，不包括！

A：I see.
我知道了！

B：Would you like to buy it?
你要買嗎？

A：No, I'll pass this time.
不要，我這次不買。

同義例句 --

例 No, thanks.
不要，謝謝！

例 Not for this time.
這次先不要（買）。

要求提供收據

Can I have a receipt?

我可以要一張收據嗎？

實用會話 --

A：How much did you say?
你說是多少錢？

B：It's $120.
是一百廿元。

A：OK. I'll take it.
好，我要買！

B：Sure. How would you like to pay?
好的！你要怎麼付款？

A：Cash, please. Can I have a receipt?
用現金，謝謝！我可以要一張收據嗎？

B：Sure, wait a moment, please.
好的！請稍等！

要求包裝

Could you wrap it up for me?

你能幫我打包嗎？

實用會話 --

A：I want to buy two of these.
　　我要買這兩件。

B：OK.
　　好的！

A：Could you wrap it up for me?
　　你能幫我打包嗎？

B：Of course. Would you wait for a second?
　　好的！能請你稍等一下嗎？

同義例句 --

例 Could you pack it for me?
　　可以幫我裝起來嗎？

例 I'd like to wrap this up.
　　我想要打包起來。

例 Please wrap this up for me.
　　請幫我把這個包起來。

134

禮品包裝

Would you wrap it as a present?

你可以包裝它成禮物嗎？

A：What do you think, sir?
　　先生，你覺得呢？

B：I'll take it.
　　我要買！

A：Sure.
　　好的！

B：Would you wrap it as a present?
　　你可以包裝它成禮物嗎？

A：I'm sorry, sir, but we don't have this service.
　　抱歉，先生，但是我們沒有這項服務。

同義例句------------------------------------

例 Could you gift-wrap it?
　　你能幫我打包成禮品嗎？

特殊包裝

Would you put them in a box?

你可以把它們放進盒子裡嗎？

實用會話------------------------------------

A：Would you put them in a box?
　　你可以把它們放進盒子裡嗎？

B：Of course, sir. Would you wait for a second?
　　當然可以的，先生！能請你稍等一下嗎？

同義例句 -

例 May I have a box to pack it?
　　我可以要一個箱子來裝它嗎？

例 I want it in a box.
　　我要把它裝在盒子裡。

例 Can I have it wrapped in a plastic bag?
　　可以用塑膠袋包裝嗎？

例 Please wrap it with paper.
　　請用紙包裝。

例 Could you wrap the book in brown paper?
　　你可以用牛皮紙把書包好嗎？

例 Will you wrap them up separately?
　　能請你幫我把他們分開包裝嗎？

例 May I have an extra bag?
　　能多給我一個袋子嗎？

已購買的商品有問題　　　　　　　　　　　MP3 135

I've found some defects in this product.

我發覺這個商品有瑕疵。

實用會話 -

A：May I help you?
　　需要我幫忙嗎？

B：I've found some defects in this product.
我發覺這個商品有瑕疵。

A：Would you like to have a refund?
你要辦理退款嗎？

B：Yes, please.
是的，麻煩你囉！

同義例句 --

例 There is a stain on this wallet.
這個皮夾上有一個污點。

相關例句 --

例 Could I return it if I don't like it?
如果我不喜歡，能退還嗎？

換貨成其他品牌

May I exchange it for another brand?
我可以換成其他的牌子嗎？

實用會話 --

A：I'd like to have a refund.
我要換貨。

B：Sure. May see your receipt?
好的！我可以看你的收據嗎？

A：Here you are. May I exchange it for another brand?
在這裡！我可以換成其他的牌子嗎？

B：Of course.
　　可以！

A：Is that one the same price?
　　那個是一樣的價錢嗎？

B：Yes, it is.
　　是的！

相關例句--

例 Could I exchange this for a different one?
　　我可以用這個換其他不同的(商品)嗎？

 退換貨　　　　　　　　　　　　　　MP3 136

I'd like to have a refund.

我要辦理退款。

 實用會話--

A：May I help you?
　　需要我幫忙嗎？

B：I'd like to have a refund.
　　我要辦理退款。

A：No problem, sir. May I see your receipt?
　　沒問題的，先生！可以給我看你的收據嗎？

B：Sure, here you are.
　　好，在這裡！

 同義例句--

例 Can I have a refund?
　　我可以退款嗎？

例 I'll take a refund.
我要辦理退款。

例 May I have a refund on this?
這個能退貨嗎？

例 I'd like to return this.
我要退貨。

其他費用

Will you charge for delivery?
你們會收運費嗎？

實用會話 --

A：Are those all washable?
那些都是可以水洗的嗎？

B：Yes. How do you like it?
是的！你喜歡嗎？

A：I don't really know... It looks nice... but ... How about $210?
不知道耶，看起來不錯…但是…兩百一十元賣不賣？

B：Deal.
成交！

A：Great. By the way, will you charge for delivery?
太好了！對了，你們會收運費嗎？

找錯錢 137

I think you gave me the wrong change.

我覺得你找錯錢了喔！

A：OK. I'll take it.

好，我要買！

B：How would you like to pay?

你要怎麼付款？

A：Cash, please.

用現金，謝謝！

B：Here is the change.

零錢在這裡！

A：I think you gave me the wrong change.

我覺得你找錯錢了喔！

B：Lets see... Sorry, my mistake.

我看看…抱歉，我弄錯了！

相關例句 --

例 I'm afraid I've been short-changed.

你好像少找我錢了！

例 I gave you a twenty not a ten.

我是給了你廿元，不是十元。

Chapter 7

和警察打交道

English Travel around the World

警察要求看證件　MP3 138

Identification, please.
證件給我。

A：Yes, officer?
　　警官，有事嗎？

B：Identification, please.
　　證件給我。

A：Sorry, officer, I've left my passport at the hotel.
　　抱歉，警官，我把護照放在飯店裡了！

B：I'm afraid you've broken the law.
　　你恐怕已經違法了！

同義例句

例 Show me your ID.
　　給我看證件。

例 Can I see your identification, please?
　　我可以看一下你的證件嗎？

例 Do you bring any identifications?
　　有帶任何的證件嗎？

例 Where is your ID card?
　　你的身分證呢？

相關例句

例 I don't have any ID with me.
　　我沒有帶任何的證件。

提供證件

Can I show you my international driver's license?

我可以給你看我的國際駕照嗎？

實用會話 --

A：What's wrong?
怎麼啦？

B：Can I see your identification, please?
我可以看一下你的證件嗎？

A：Can I show you my international driver's license?
我可以給你看我的國際駕照嗎？

B：Of course.
當然可以！

相關例句 --

例 Let me see your passport and visa.
讓我看看你的護照和簽證。

例 What is your passport number?
你的護照號碼是幾號？

被質疑證件的合法性　 139

This is not your ID card.

這不是你的身分證。

實用會話 --

A：Please show me your passport.
　　請出示你的護照。

B：Here you are, officer.
　　警官，在這裡！

A：This is not your ID card.
　　這不是你的身分證。

B：It's mine.
　　這是我的。

A：See? I've changed my hair style.
　　瞧？我換了髮型了！

同義例句 --

例 You are showing me the false identification, aren't you?
　　你給我的是假的證件，對吧？

例 Are you sure this is your ID card?
　　你確定這是你的身分證嗎？

證件過期

Your passport expired.
你的護照過期了。

A：Please show me your passport.
請出示你的護照。

B：Here you are, officer.
警官，在這裡！

A：Your passport expired.
你的護照過期了。

B：Really? That must be a mistake.
真的？一定是弄錯了吧！

例 Your license will expire tomorrow.
你的駕照明天就要過期了。

例 This certificate is valid for three months.
這個證件有效期是三個月。

例 Your driver's license has expired, so it is invalid.
你的駕照過期了，所以這是無效的。

違法事件 140

Did I break the law?

我有犯法嗎？

A：What's going on here? Did I break the law?
　　這裡發生什麼事了？我有犯法嗎？

B：It is forbidden to do so in the USA.
　　在美國禁止這樣的行為。

同義例句 --

例 I'm afraid you already broke the law.
　　恐怕你已經違法了。

例 It's illegal.
　　這是違規的。

例 You have broken the law.
　　你已經違法了。

相關例句 --

例 It's against the law.
　　這是違法的。

例 It's still against the law.
　　那還是違法的。

同義例句 --

You're suspected of homicide.

你涉有殺人罪嫌。

實用會話 --

A：Officer, what did I do?
　　警官，我做了什麼？

B：You're suspected of homicide.
　　你涉有殺人罪嫌。

A：Me? It must be a mistake.
　　是我嗎？一定是誤會！

B：You'll have to come with us to the station.
　　你要跟我們來警局一趟。

A：But... but why?
　　但是，為什麼？

同義例句 --

例 You have committed a crime.
　 你犯罪了。

例 You will be charged with possessing illegal drugs.
　 你將以持有毒品被起訴。

罰款

MP3 141

You have to pay a fine.

你會被罰款。

實用會話 -

A：If you smoke in the MRT, you have to pay a fine.
如果在捷運站內抽煙，你就要被罰款。

B：I'm really sorry. I won't do it again.
我真的很抱歉。我不會再這麼做了。

A：Sorry, I have to give you a ticket.
抱歉，我必須開你罰單。

B：I'm sorry, but I didn't do it on purpose.
抱歉，我不是故意這麼做的。

相關例句 -

例 Riding without wearing a helmet is a five hundred dollars fine.
騎機車未戴安全帽，罰五佰元。

例 You are fined three hundred dollars.
你被罰款三百元。

例 This is your ticket.
這是你的罰單。

例 I'm going to write you a ticket.
我要開罰單給你。

警察表明身分

Police!

（我們是）警察！

A：Who is it?
是誰？

B：Police!
（我們是）警察！

（開門後）

A：What did I do?
我有做什麼事嗎？

B：Freeze!
不准動！

A：Hey, easy. Did I break the law?
嘿，冷靜點！我有犯法嗎？

警察提出要求

Hands up!

手舉起來！

A：Hands up!
手舉起來！

B：OK. I'll do what you said.
好！我會照著你說的做。

同義例句 --------------------------------

例 On your knees!
跪下！

例 Get down!
蹲下！

例 Get down on the ground!
趴在地上！

例 Get back!
退後！

例 Come here!
過來！

例 Get into the car.
上車。

例 Turn around slowly!
慢慢地轉過身來！

被要求看見雙手

Let me see your hands.

讓我看到你的雙手。

實用會話 --------------------------------

A：What happened?
發生什麼事了？

B：Let me see your hands.
讓我看到你的雙手。

A：Sure. I'll do what you said.
　　好！我會照著你說的做。

B：Are you David Jones?
　　你是大衛・瓊斯嗎？

A：Yes, it's me.
　　是的，我就是！

同義例句 ---

例 Put your hands where I can see.
　 把你的手放在我可以看得見的地方。

例 Put your hands on your head.
　 把雙手放在頭上。

例 Take your hands out of your pockets slowly.
　 慢慢地把你的手從口袋裡拿出來。

服從警察的要求　　　　　　　　　　　　　　MP3 143

I'll do what you said.

我會照做。

實用會話 ---

A：Calm down. Drop your weapon!
　　冷靜點！放下武器！

B：Easy. I'm going to drop it down.
　　不要緊張！我要放下了。

A：Stay where you are.
　　待在原地不要動！

B：No problem. I'll do what you said.
沒問題。我會照做的。

想知道發生何事

What did I do?

我有做了什麼事嗎？

實用會話 --

A：Freeze!
不准動！

B：What? What did I do? It must be a mistake.
什麼？我做了什麼事？一定弄錯了。

A：Let me see your hands.
讓我看到你的雙手。

B：Sure.
好！

同義例句 --

例 What happened?
發生了什麼事？

例 What's going on?
怎麼了？

例 Hey, what's the problem?
嘿，怎麼回事？

例 Don't shoot. I did nothing.
不要開槍。我什麼事都沒做！

相關例句 --

例 Halt or I'll shoot!
不要動,不然我要開槍!

例 Don't move!
不准動!

例 Stay where you are.
站在原地。

被逮捕時

I want to see my lawyer.
我要見我的律師。

實用會話 --

A : I'm going to put handcuffs on you.
我要把你銬上手銬。

B : Hey, you can't do this to me. Easy. It hurts.
嘿,你不能這麼對我。輕一點,很痛的!

A : Don't move! You're under arrest!
不准動!你被捕了!

B : You have no right to arrest me.
你們沒有權力逮捕我。

A : We have an arrest warrant.
我們有拘票!

B : I want to see my lawyer.
我要見我的律師。

相關例句 ---

例 We can keep you in lock-up for about twenty-four hours.
我們可以把你拘留廿四小時。

搜索　　　　　　　　　　　　　　　　　　　MP3 144

Where is your warrant?
你們的搜索令呢？

實用會話 ---

A：Police. Let us in.
我們是警察！讓我們進去！

B：Where is your warrant?
你們的搜索令呢？

A：This is a warrant issued by a court.
這是法院發出的搜查令。

B：That must be a mistake.
一定是誤會！

A：You have the right to remain silent.
你有權保持緘默。

相關例句 ---

例 We are police officers. Let us in.
我們是警察。讓我們進去。

例 We have a search warrant.
我們有搜索票！

例 We have a warrant to search your house.
我們有搜索令可以搜查你的房子。

同義例句 --

例 Do you understand your rights?
你是否了解你的權利？

例 Anything you tell the police may be used against you later in court.
你對警察所言會當成呈堂證供。

例 You don't have to say anything.
你不必說任何事情。

提出捍衛權益的要求   **MP3 145**

I want to make a phone call.
我要打電話。

實用會話 --

A：You're under arrest.
你被捕了！

B：You can't do this to me.
你不能這麼對我！

A：You are accused of murder.
你被指控犯了殺人罪。

B：I want to make a phone call.
我要打電話。

同義例句 --

例 I want to see our ambassador.
我要見我們的大使。

例 I want to see my parents.
我要見我的父母。

報案

There's a robbery at the First Avenue.

在第一大道發生搶案。

實用會話 --

A：Police Operator 312. What do you want to report?
警用專線，我是312號服務人員。你要報什麼案件？

B：I want to report a robbery.
我要報案發生搶案！

A：Where is it?
在哪裡？

B：There's a robbery at the First Avenue.
在第一大道發生搶案。

同義例句 --

例 I just had a car accident.
我剛剛發生車禍。

例 There is a fire in my building at the First Street.
在第一街我住的大樓發生火災。

至警察局報案 **MP3** 146

I want to report a robbery.
我要報一件搶案。

實用會話 --

A：How can I help?
　　需要我幫忙嗎？

B：I want to report a robbery.
　　我要報案發生搶案。

A：All right. Please fill out this form.
　　好的！請填寫這份表格。

相關例句 --

例 Someone broke into my house.
　　有人闖進我家。

 被攻擊

I was assaulted.
我被攻擊了。

實用會話 --

A：You're through to the police. How can I help you?
　　這是警察專線，需要我幫忙嗎？

B：Please come. Please come quick.
　　請派人過來，請快一點！

A：Calm down, madam. What happened?
　　冷靜點，女士。發生什麼事了？

B：I was assaulted. He's going to kill me.
　　我被攻擊了。他要殺我！

A：What's your name?
　　妳叫什麼名字？

同義例句 --

例 He beat me for no reason.
　　他毫無理由就打我。

例 He suddenly assaulted me.
　　他突然攻擊我。

例 Someone pointed a gun at me.
　　有一個人拿槍對著我。

例 Someone attacked me.
　　有一個人攻擊我。

例 There was a man tried to rape me.
　　有一個男人企圖強暴我。

物品被搶　　　　　　　　　　　　　　　　　　　　MP3 147

He snatched away my bag.

他搶走我的袋子。

 實用會話 --

A：Help.
　　救命啊！

B：What happened to you?
發生什麼事了？

A：He snatched away my bag.
他搶走我的袋子。

B：Do you know what he was wearing?
你知道他穿什麼衣服嗎？

A：No, I'm not sure. It happened so fast. All I know...
he had a tattoo on his neck.
不知道，我不太確定！發生得太快了！我只知道他的脖子上有
刺青。

同義例句 -

例 Two men just robbed me.
剛才我被兩個人搶劫。

例 They said nothing, and took away my bags.
他們沒有說什麼，就拿走我的背包。

相關例句 -

例 Someone stole my suitcase.
我的行李被扒走了。

物品遺失

I have lost my bag.

我把袋子弄丟了。

實用會話 -

A：What do you want to report?
你要報什麼案件？

B：I have lost my bag.
　　我把袋子弄丟了。

A：When did it happen?
　　什麼時候發生的？

B：I have no idea. I think I left it in the park.
　　我不知道！我覺得好像丟在公園了！

同義例句 -------------------------------------

例 I can't find my passport.
　　我找不到我的護照。

例 I left my bag in a cab.
　　我把袋子遺失在計程車上。

例 I lost my wallet somewhere in the park.
　　我在公園的某個地方遺失了我的皮夾。

孩子失蹤　　　　　　　　　　　 148

I can't find my kids.

我找不到我的孩子們。

實用會話 -------------------------------------

A：Police Operator 122. What's your emergency?
　　警用專線，我是122號服務人員。有什麼緊急事件嗎？

B：I can't find my kids.
　　我找不到我的孩子們。

A：Do you have any pictures of your kids?
　　你有孩子們的任何照片嗎？

同義例句 --

例 My boy was kidnapped.
我的兒子被綁架了。

例 My kid was missing.
我的孩子失蹤了。

警方的處理

We'll take care of everything.

我們會處理一切的。

實用會話 --

A：Police operator 122.
警用專線，我是 122 號服務人員。

B：A guy just robbed me. He stuck a gun in my face and took everything.
有一個男人搶我！他用搶指著我的臉然後搶走我的東西！

A：Where is that guy now?
那傢伙現在在哪裡？

B：I don't know. I'm so scared.
我不知道！我好害怕。

A：Don't be afraid. We'll take care of everything.
不用害怕！我們會處理一切的。

同義例句 --

例 We'll do our best.
我們會盡力。

例 We'll help you.
我們會幫你的。

警方將派人處理 MP3 149

We'll send an officer there.

我們會派警察過去。

 實用會話 --

A : Police operator 122. What's your
emergency?
警用專線，我是122號服務人員。有什麼緊急事件嗎？

B : There is a murder in my building.
我的大樓發生謀殺案。

A : We'll send an officer there right now.
我們會馬上派警員過去。

 同義例句 --

例 We'll be there soon.
我們很快就會過去。

例 Police are on their way.
警方過去了！

例 I'll send the police to you. OK?
我派警員過去，好嗎？

目擊案件發生

I witnessed a traffic accident.

我目睹了交通事故。

實用會話

A：Did you witness the accident?
你有目擊意外發生嗎？

B：Yes, I witnessed a traffic accident.
有，我目睹了交通事故。

A：What did you see?
你看見什麼？

B：There's a black wagon.
有一台黑色的貨車。

同義例句

例 I was standing right there.
我就站在那裡。

例 I was talking to that victim at that moment.
我當時和那個被害人在說話。

相關例句

例 I saw nothing.
我什麼都沒有看到。

描述犯人的面貌、衣著　 MP3 150

His face is thin and tanned.

他的面孔瘦削，曬得很黑。

實用會話 --------------------------------

A：What did the suspect look like?
　　嫌犯長什麼樣子？

B：His face is thin and tanned.
　　他的面孔瘦削，曬得很黑。

A：Can you identify him?
　　你能指認他嗎？

B：Yes, I recognize him.
　　可以，我認得他。

同義例句 --------------------------------

例 He has long brown hair.
　　他有一頭褐色長髮。

例 He has black eyes.
　　他的眼睛是黑色的。

例 It's a guy in white.
　　是個穿白衣的男人。

例 It's a black in red.
　　是個穿紅衣的黑人。

例 He is about forties in red shirt.
　　他大約四十多歲，身穿紅襯衫。

描述犯人的體型

He's very tall.

他很高。

 實用會話 --------------------------------

A：Can you give me a description?
　　可以形容一下對方的樣子嗎？

B：He's very tall, about six feet tall, I guess.
　　他很高，我猜他大概有六呎高。

同義例句 --------------------------------

例 He's a tall and fat guy.
　　他是個又高又胖的男人。

例 He's a tall man in his mid forties.
　　他身材高大，大約四十五歲左右。

相關例句 --------------------------------

例 He's about twenties.
　　他大約二十多歲。

例 He looks in his mid thirties.
　　他看起來三十五歲左右。

例 He's young.
　　他很年輕。

例 He's a teenager.
　　他是個十幾歲的青少年。

猜測犯人身分　　　　　MP3 151

He's white.

他是白人。

A：Is the suspect white?
　　嫌疑犯是白人嗎？

B：Yes, he's a white.
　　是的，他是白人。

例 He's a white male.
　　他是一位白人男性。

例 She's a black female.
　　她是一位黑人女性。

例 He's an Asian with beard.
　　他是一個蓄著山羊鬍的亞洲人。

案件發生的地點

It's in front of the post office.

就在郵局前面。

A：I want to report a robbery.
　　我要報案發生搶案。

B：Where did the incident occur?
這件事是在什麼地方發生的？

A：It's in front of the post office.
就在郵局前面。

同義例句 ---

例 Inside the MRT.
在捷運站裡面。

例 At the bank.
在銀行。

例 At a restaurant.
在一家餐廳。

案件發生的時間 152

It's about 10 am.

大約早上十點鐘。

實用會話 ---

A：What time did this accident occur?
這件事故是什麼時候發生的？

B：It's about 10 am.
大約早上十點鐘。

同義例句 ---

例 At night.
在晚上（發生）。

例 It happened when I made breakfast.
當我做早餐的時候發生的。

例 I happened after I stepped out of the building.
在我步出大樓後發生的。

被要求停車

Pull over.
靠邊停車！

實用會話 --

A：Pull over.
靠邊停車！

B：What's up, sir?
警官，有什麼事？

A：Please show me your ID.
請給我看你的證件。

B：Sure. Here you are.
好的，在這裡！

同義例句 --

例 Turn off the car.
把車子熄火！

被警察臨檢

What's wrong?
有什麼不對嗎？

A：Pull over.
　　停車！

B：What's wrong?
　　有什麼不對嗎？

A：May I see your ID?
　　請出示你的身分證件。

B：Is there anything wrong? I didn't violate any laws.
　　有問題嗎？我沒有犯法！

同義例句 --

例 What happened?
　　發生什麼事了？

例 What did I do?
　　我做了什麼？

例 Did I do something against the law?
　　我違規了嗎？

例 Am I in trouble?
　　我有什麼麻煩了嗎？

交通臨檢

This is a traffic check.

這是交通臨檢。

實用會話 --

A：Something wrong, officer?
　　警官，發生什麼事了？

B：This is a traffic check.
　　這是交通臨檢。

同義例句 --

例 This is a routine examination.
　　這是例行的檢查。

例 This is a routine job.
　　這是例行的工作。

臨檢的原因

MP3 154

We're doing a vehicle check.

我們正在做車輛臨檢。

實用會話 --

A：Did I do something wrong?
　　我有做錯事嗎？

B：No. We're doing a vehicle check.
　　沒有，我們正在做車輛臨檢。

同義例句 --

例 We're having a traffic security check.
我們正在做交通安全臨檢。

例 We're looking for a criminal.
我們正在搜尋一名罪犯。

例 We're looking for an escapee from the prison.
我們正在搜尋一名逃獄犯。

被要求配合臨檢

Please roll down your window.
請搖下車窗。

實用會話 --

A：Please roll down your window.
請搖下車窗。

B：Yes, officer?
警官，有什麼事嗎？

A：Step outside, please.
請下車。

相關例句 --

例 Keep your hands on the steering wheel.
把手放在方向盤上。

例 Just remain inside your car.
請留在車內。

例 Were you drinking tonight?
你今晚有喝酒嗎？

搜查車子　 **155**

We need to search your car.

我們要搜查你的車子。

A：Pull over.
　　停車。

B：What's wrong, officer?
　　警官，發生什麼事了？

A：We need to search your car.
　　我們要搜查你的車子。

B：What happened?
　　發生什麼事了？

A：It is just a routine checkpoint, please do not be alarmed.
　　只是例行盤檢，請不用緊張！

同義例句 --

例 Please open your trunk.
　　請打開你的行李廂。

例 Please show me your storage compartment.
　　請讓我看你的置物箱。

例 Let me see your trunk.
　　請讓我看你的行李廂。

例 May I see your trunk?
　　我可以檢查你的行李廂嗎？

告知自己要拿證件

May I look for my ID?

我可以找一下我的證件嗎？

實用會話 --

A：I need to see your driver's license.
　　我必須看一下你的駕照。

B：May I look for my ID?
　　我可以找一下我的證件嗎？

A：Please do it.
　　請便。

同義例句 --

例 I'll look for my ID.
　 我要找一下我的證件。

看證件的原因

 MP3 156

What for?

為什麼？

實用會話 --

A：Please pull over your car and step out of the
　　vehicle. May I see your driver's license?
　　請停車，下車。我可以看你的駕照嗎？

B：What for?
　　為什麼？

A：You were going the wrong way on a one-way street.
你在單行道上逆向行駛。

B：I won't make the same mistake next time.
我下次不會再犯了！

A：I am sorry, sir. Please sign here for your ticket.
抱歉，先生，請在罰單上簽字。

同義例句 --

例 Why?
為什麼？

例 How come?
為什麼？

確認警官的身分

May I know your badge number?

你的警徽號碼是幾號？

實用會話 --

A：Police. Don't move.
我是警察！不准動！

B：What's going on here?
發生什麼事了？

A：I need to ask you a few questions.
我需要問你一些問題。

B：Why? I don't even know you. May I know your badge number?
為什麼？我連你是誰我都不知道。你的警徽號碼是幾號？

A：Sure. My name is David Johnson.
好！我是大衛・強生。

詢問警察的行為

What are you checking with your computer?

你在用電腦查什麼？

A：What are you checking with your computer?
你在用電腦查什麼？

B：To check and see if you are a reported missing person or a wanted criminal.
看看你是不是通報失蹤人口或懸賞的罪犯。

證件已經過期

Your driver's license already expired.

你的駕照已經過期了。

A：Your driver's license, please.
給我你的駕照。

B：Here it is.
在這裡。

A：Your driver's license already expired.
你的駕照已經過期了。

同義例句 --

例 Your license will expire tomorrow.
你的駕照明天要過期了。

例 Your license expired on the last day of September.
你的駕照在九月卅日就過期了。

例 Your vehicle registration will expire on September.
你的行照今年九月就要到期了喔！

例 Your vehicle insurance expired last month.
你的車險上個月過期了。

為證件過期找藉口　 158

Your license expired last week.

你的駕照在上星期就過期了。

實用會話 --

A：Your license expired last week.
　　你的駕照在上星期就過期了。

B：Really? Let me see.
　　真的？我瞧瞧。

A：I'm going to write you a ticket.
　　我要開罰單給你。

B：But it's only a few days out of date, officer.
　　警官，只有過期幾天啊！

同義例句 --

例 I really don't know about it, officer.
警官，我真的不知道這件事。

被質疑不是車主

Is this your car, sir?

先生，這是你的車子嗎？

實用會話 -

A：What's wrong?
怎麼回事？

B：Is this your car, sir?
先生，這是你的車子嗎？

A：Of course, officer. It's my car.
當然是啊，警官。 這是我的車子。

B：May I see your driver's license and vehicle registration?
請給我看你的駕照和行照！

A：Sure, here you are.
好的，在這裡！

同義例句 -

例 Do you own this car?
你是車主嗎？

例 May I see the owner's ID for the vehicle?
我可以看這輛車的車主身分證件嗎？

車籍資料　 MP3 159

Here is my vehicle registration.

這是我的行照。

實用會話 --

A：Here is my vehicle registration.
　　這是我的行照。

B：This is not the vehicle registration of this motor-bike.
　　這不是這輛機車的行照。

同義例句 --

例 This vehicle registration number doesn't belong to this car.
　　這個行照號碼不是這輛車的。

被質疑為贓車

Where did you get this car?

你這輛車哪裡來的？

 實用會話 --

A：Yes, sir?
　　警官，有什麼事？

B：Where did you get this car?
　　你這輛車哪裡來的？

A：I rent this car.
　我租的。

B：I'm afraid this is a stolen car.
　這恐怕是一輛失竊的車。

A：A stolen car? It can't be.
　這是失竊的車子？不可能啊！

車子的所有權　　　　　　　　　　　　　　**MP3** 160

It's my car.
是我的車子。

A：Is the 4545 GF your car?
　4545 GF 是你的車嗎？

B：Yes, it's my car.
　對，是我的車子。

A：May I see your driver's license and vehicle
　registration?
　請給我看你的駕照和行照！

例 I rent it.
　我租的。

例 It's not my vehicle.
　這不是我的車。

例 Mine is over there, 4245 GF.
　我的車子是在那裡，是 4245 GF。

Chapter · **8**

尋求協助

English Travel around the World

尋求協助

MP3 161

Please do me a favor.

請幫我一個忙。

實用會話 --

A：Please do me a favor.
　　請幫我一個忙。

B：What is it?
　　要幫什麼忙？

A：Can you keep an eye on my bag, please? Nature's calling.
　　可以幫我看一下袋子嗎？我要去上廁所！

B：Sure. Will it be long?
　　好啊！會很久嗎？

A：No. I just want to use the bathroom.
　　不會！我只是去洗手間！

B：Go ahead. It'll be safe with me.
　　去吧！我來幫你看著！

同義例句 --

例 Give me a hand, please.
　　請幫我一個忙。

例 Would you please help me?
　　能請你幫我一個忙嗎？

例 I need your help.
　　我需要你的幫忙。

提供幫忙

I'll get this bag for you.

我幫你拿袋子。

A：Oh, my!
　　喔，天啊！

B：I'll get this bag for you.
　　我幫你拿袋子。

A：Thank you so much.
　　非常感謝你。

B：No problem.
　　不客氣！

相關例句

例 Let me help you with it.
　　我來幫你！

例 Would you like me to get you a cab?
　　需要我幫你叫計程車嗎？

詢問是否需要提供幫忙　　　　　　　　 162

Can I help you?

需要幫忙嗎？

A：Can I help you?
　　需要幫忙嗎？

B：Yes. Could you get that bag for me?
　　是的。可以幫我拿那個袋子嗎？

A：Sure. Here you are.
　　好啊！給你！

B：Thank you so much.
　　非常感謝你！

A：You're welcome.
　　不客氣！

同義例句 --

例 Do you need any help?
　　需要幫忙嗎？

例 Do you want me to help you?
　　希望我幫你嗎。

例 Is there anything I can do?
　　有沒有什麼我可以做的？

例 Is there something I can do?
　　有沒有我可以做的事？

客氣地接受幫助

If it's not too much trouble, I'd like some help.

如果不麻煩，我需要你的幫忙。

 實用會話 --

A：Is there anything I can do?
　　有沒有什麼我可以做的？

B：If it's not too much trouble, I'd like some help.
如果不麻煩，我需要你的幫忙。

A：It's no trouble at all. I'll carry this suitcase for you.
一點都不會麻煩。我來幫你搬這個行李。

B：It's very nice of you.
你真好心！

例 If you wouldn't mind, I'd need your help.
如果你不介意的話，我需要你的幫忙。

提出要求

May I use your telephone?

我能借用你的電話嗎？

A：What can I do for you?
有什麼需要我協助嗎？

B：May I use your telephone?
我能借用你的電話嗎？

A：Sure, go ahead.
好，你用吧！

B：Thanks a lot.
多謝啦！

例 May I have it?
可以給我嗎？

例 May I take a look at it?
　　我可以看一下嗎？

例 May I use this?
　　我可以使用嗎？

例 Could I touch this one?
　　我可以摸一下這個嗎？

例 Is this seat taken?
　　這張椅子有人坐嗎？

例 Can you keep an eye on my bag?
　　可以幫我看著袋子嗎？

提出問題

Do you know what it is?
你知道這是什麼嗎？

實用會話 --

A : What can I do for you?
　　有什麼需要我協助嗎？

B : Do you know what it is?
　　你知道這是什麼嗎？

A : It's a horse.
　　這是一匹馬。

B : A horse? It looks like a donkey.
　　這是馬？好像驢子喔！

同義例句 --

例 Do you know how to say it in English?
　　你知道用英文要怎麼說它嗎？

要不要搭便車 **164**

Do you want a ride?

要不要搭便車？

實用會話 ------------------------------------

A：Good afternoon, Eric.
艾瑞克，午安。

B：hi, Sandy. Do you want a ride?
嗨，珊蒂。要不要搭便車？

A：If you wouldn't mind, could you give me a ride home?
如果你不介意的話，可以讓我搭便車回家嗎？

B：No, not at all. Get in.
不會，沒關係！上車吧！

沒聽清楚對方的話

Excuse me?

你說什麼？

實用會話 ------------------------------------

A：Excuse me?
你說什麼？

B：I said "Do you want me to help you?"
我說「你要我幫忙嗎？」

A：No, thanks. I can handle this by myself.
不用，謝謝！我可以自己來！

同義例句 ---

例 I beg your pardon?
你說什麼？

例 Pardon?
請再說一次。

例 What was that?
什麼？

例 I didn't hear what you said.
我沒聽見你說什麼。

例 I'm sorry I didn't catch what you said.
抱歉，我沒聽清楚你說什麼。

例 What did you just say?
你剛剛說什麼？

請對方再說一次

MP3 165

Pardon?

請再說一次。

 實用會話 --

A：Please move over.
請移過去一點。

B：Pardon?
請再說一次。

A：I said "Move over."
我說移過去一點。

B：Sure.
好！

危急時刻的呼救

Help!

救命啊！

 實用會話 --

A：Help!
　　救命啊！

B：What happened?
　　發生什麼事了？

A：Call an ambulance.
　　叫救護車！

同義例句 --

例 Anybody here?
　　有人在嗎？

例 Somebody, help me.
　　來人啊！救救我！

相關例句 --

例 That tall guy robbed my backpack.
　　那個高個子搶了我的背包。

例 Fire.
　　發生火災了！

例 There is a boy in the river.
　　有一個小男孩掉入河裡了！

例 I've see two cars crash into a truck.
　　我看見兩輛車衝撞一輛貨車！

要求報警　　　　　　　　　　　　　　　　　　　MP3 166

Please call the police for me.

請幫我叫警察。

實用會話 --

A：Oh, my God.
　　喔，我的天啊！

B：Are you OK?
　　你還好吧？

A：Please call the police for me.
　　請幫我叫警察。

B：Just stay here. I'll get someone to help you.
　　待在這裡！我找人來幫你！

同義例句 --

例 Please call 911.
　　請報警。(911 為美國的報警電話)

問路

Where is the Custom Tour Center?

「旅客旅遊中心」在哪裡？

實用會話 --

A：Excuse me. Where is the Custom Tour Center?
　　請問，「旅客旅遊中心」在哪裡？

B：It's right on the corner of the first street.
　　就在第一街的角落。

A：I see. Thank you so much.
我知道了。非常感謝你。

同義例句 -------------------------------

例 Where's the museum?
博物館在哪裡？

例 Where's the duty-free shop?
免稅店在哪裡？

例 Where's the restroom?
洗手間在哪兒？

例 Where's the nearest police station?
離這兒最近的警察局在哪裡？

例 Do you know of any police stations near here?
你知道這附近有任何警察局嗎？

請求指示方向 167

Would you show me how to get there?

可以告訴我如何去那裡嗎？

實用會話 -------------------------------

A：Do you want me to help you?
要我幫你嗎？

B：Yes. Would you show me how to get there?
是的！可以告訴我如何去那裡？

A：Let's see. Turn right and you will see it.
我想想！右轉就會看到。

B：Thanks a lot.

多謝啦！

 同義例句 --------------------------------

例 How do I get to the museum?

我要怎麼去博物館？

例 How do I get to the City Hall?

我要怎麼去市府？

例 Could you give me directions to the City Hall?

可以告訴我去市府的方向嗎？

例 What direction should I follow to get to the City Hall?

哪一個方向可以去市府？

說明方向

Go straight for two blocks.

一直走，過兩條街。

實用會話 --------------------------------

A：Is this the way to the railway station?

這是去火車站的路嗎？

B：No. You're going the wrong way.

不是，你走錯路了。

A：Where is the railway station?

火車站在哪裡？

B：Go straight for two blocks.

一直走，過兩條街。

同義例句 --------------------------------

例 Turn right and go straight ahead.
左轉再直走。

例 Go through the door.
穿過門就到了。

例 It's on your left side.
在你的左手邊

例 Make a right at the traffic light.
在紅綠燈右轉。

例 Turn right at the first traffic light.
在第一個紅綠燈右轉。

例 Go straight ahead until the traffic light and it's on your right side.
直走到紅綠燈，就在你的右手邊。

迷路 168

Yes, I'm lost.

是的，我迷路了。

A：May I help you?
需要我幫忙嗎？

B：Yes, I'm lost.
是的，我迷路了。

A：Where do you want to go?
你想去哪裡？

B：Is there a police station near here?
這附近有警察局嗎？

A：Yes, there is. Go straight ahead and you will see it on your right side.

有，在那兒。一直往前走，你就會看到在你的右手邊。

同義例句 --

例 I don't know where I am.

我不知道我現在身在何處。

例 What street am I on?

我現在在哪條街上？

例 Where am I on this map?

我在地圖上的什麼地方？

例 Where am I?

我在哪兒呢？

指出所在地

You're right here, near the station.

你在這兒，在車站附近。

實用會話 --

A：Excuse me. I'm lost.

抱歉，我迷路了。

B：Let's see... You're right here, near the station.

我看看…你在這兒，在車站附近。

A：I see. Is it close to the museum?

我知道了！離博物館很近嗎？

B：The Metropolitan Museum of Art?

是大都會博物館嗎？

A：That's right.
　　沒錯！

B：Yes, it's about five minutes' walk.
　　是啊，大概五分鐘路程。

指出相關地點的所在地　　　　　　　　 169

It's next to the coffee shop.
在咖啡館的旁邊。

 -

A：Do you need any help?
　　需要幫忙嗎？

B：Yes, I'm lost. Do you know where the museum is?
　　是的，我迷路了。你知道博物館在哪裡嗎？

A：It's across from the City Hall.
　　在市府的對面。

同義例句 -

例 It's next to the coffee shop.
　　在咖啡館的旁邊。

例 It's on the opposite side of the City Hall.
　　正對著市府。

例 It's between the bookstore and the station.
　　在書店和車站之間。

例 It's on this side of the church.
　　在教堂的這一邊。

例 It's at the end of this street.
　　在這條街道的盡頭。

明顯的地標

What are the landmarks around the station?

車站附近有沒有明顯的建築物？

實用會話 --

A：You'll see it on your right side.
你就會看到在你的右手邊。

B：What are the landmarks around the station?
車站附近有沒有明顯的建築物？

A：There is a red building next to the station.
車站旁有一棟紅色的建築物。

B：I see. Thank you so much.
我知道了！非常感謝你！

車子故障打電話求救 170

I don't know if you can help me.

不知道你可以幫我嗎？

實用會話 --

A：Hello, Speed Service Station.
喂！這是 Speed 服務站！

B：Hi. I don't know if you can help me. My car's broken down.
嗨。不知道你可以幫我嗎？我的車子拋錨了！

A：We have 24-hour service. Where are you?
我們有廿四小時服務。你在哪裡？

B：I'm on US 31, just south of Hopeville. I just past the Red Café.

我在 US31 道路上，在 Hopeville 南方。我剛剛通過 Red 咖啡店。

A：I'll send a mechanic out to you. He'll be there in about 20 minutes.

我會派技工過去你那裡。他大概廿分鐘就會到。

B：Thanks.

謝謝！

車子拋錨了

My car won't start.

我的車就是發不動。

A：What happended?

發生什麼事了？

B：I have no idea... My car won't start.

我不知道耶！我的車就是發不動。

A：Let me take a look at it.

我來看一看！

B：I really appreciate it.

太感謝了！

A：No problem.

不客氣！

例 My car's broken down.

我的車壞了！

例 My car broke down on the freeway.
我的車在高速公路上拋錨了。

例 It won't start.
沒辦法發動！

例 I have a flat tire.
我的輪胎沒氣了。

例 We have a flat tire here.
我們的車爆胎了。

解決車子拋錨的問題

Could you help jump-start my car?
可以用你車上的電瓶幫我發動車子嗎？

實用會話 --

A：What can I do for you?
有什麼需要我協助嗎？

B：Could you help jump-start my car?
可以用你車上的電瓶幫我發動車子嗎？

A：OK. I'll see what I can do. It's nothing serious.
好！我來看看能幫什麼忙！不嚴重啦！

B：What happened?
怎麼了？

A：You've just run out of gas.
你沒汽油了啦！

B：Oh. Can you tow me back to the service station?
是喔！你可以幫我把車子拖回服務站嗎？

A：That's not necessary. I have a spare can of gas with me.
不用啦！我這裡有一桶汽油。

被反鎖在車外

I'm locked out of my car.
我被反鎖在車外了！

實用會話 --

A：Do you need help?
你需要幫助嗎？

B：Yes. I'm locked out of my car.
是的，我被反鎖在車外了！

A：Don't worry. I have a jimmy. Wait a moment.
不用擔心！我有帶開車門的工具。

輪胎爆胎

MP3 172

I had a flat on the way.
我在來的路上爆胎了！

實用會話 --

A：Hey, buddy. What happened to your car?
嗨，兄弟，你的車怎麼了？

B：I have no idea.
不知道耶！

A：Let's see... I think your shocks are wearing out.
我看看…你的避震器壞了！

B：Shit. I also had a flat on the way.

糟糕！我在來的路上還爆胎了！

A：Do you have a spare?

你有備胎嗎？

B：No, I don't. What should I do now?

沒有！我沒有！我該怎麼辦？

A：I'll call a tow truck for you.

我幫你打電話來拖車！

開車時發生擦撞

I didn't mean it.

我不是故意的！

 實用會話 --

A：Shit.

糟糕！

B：What seems to be the problem with your car?

你的車是哪裡有問題啊？

A：Sorry. I didn't mean it.

抱歉，我不是故意的！

同義例句 ---

例 My mistake.

是我的錯！

例 It's my fault.

是我的錯！

例 I didn't see you.

我沒有看到你！

車子加油   MP3 173

Fill'er up!

加滿油！

A：Fill'er up!
　　加滿油！

B：Should I check the tires?
　　我要幫你檢查一下輪胎嗎？

A：No, that's all for now.
　　不用，這樣就好！

B：OK, sir.
　　好的，先生！

同義例句 ----------------------------------

例 Fill'er up with unleaded.
　　加滿無鉛汽油。

例 Fill'er up with regular, pleaes.
　　請加滿一般汽油。

加滿油多少錢

What does it come to?

多少錢？

A：Fill'er up!
　　加滿！

B：All right.
　　好的。

A：What does it come to?
　　多少錢？

B：That'll be $10.
　　十元。

A：OK. Here you are.
　　好！給你！

例 How much is it?
　　多少錢？

例 How much do I owe you for the gas?
　　加汽油總共多少？

所有的費用　　　　　　　　　　　　　 174

How much do I owe you for everything?

總共多少錢？

實用會話 ---

A：Fill'er up!
　　加滿！

B：All right.
　　好的！

A：Could you check the oil and the battery?
　　可以幫我檢查機油和電瓶嗎？

B：No problem, sir.
沒問題的，先生。

A：How much do I owe you for everything?
總共多少錢？

B：With the new battery, $134.
包括新的電瓶，共一百卅四元。

同義例句 --

例 How much do I owe you for the new tire?
新的輪胎要多少錢？

檢查車況的服務

And can you take a look at my battery?

可以幫我看看我的電瓶嗎？

實用會話 --

A：Fill'er up with regular, pleaes.
請加滿一般汽油。

B：Sure.
好的！

A：And can you take a look at my battery?
可以幫我看看我的電瓶嗎？

B：Yes, sir. The battery's dead.
好的，先生。電瓶沒有電了！

同義例句 ---

例 Could you check the tires?

可以幫我檢查輪胎嗎？

例 Could you check the radiator?

可以幫我檢查散熱氣嗎？

例 Could you check the oil?

可以幫我檢查機油嗎？

例 Please check the rear window.

請幫我檢查後面的窗戶。

例 Please clean the windshield.

請幫我清洗雨刷。

拒絕加油之外的其他服務　　　　　　　　　　 MP3 175

No, thanks. I'm in a hurry.

不用，謝謝！我正在趕路。

實用會話 ---

A：Fill'er up with regular, pleaes.

請加滿一般汽油。

B：Sure. Should I take a look at your battery?

好的！要我檢查電瓶嗎？

A：No, thanks. I'm in a hurry.

不用，謝謝！我正在趕路。

B：Do you want me to take a look at the muffler?

要我幫你看看消音器嗎？

A：No, thank you. I don't have time.

不用，謝謝！我沒有時間。

接受加油之外的其他服務

Yes, please.

好的，麻煩你囉！

實用會話 --

A：Fill'er up with regular, pleaes.
請加滿一般汽油。

B：OK. Do you want to check the tires?
好的！要檢查一下輪胎嗎？

A：Yes, please. And can you check the battery too?
好的，麻煩你囉！還有，可以請你檢查一下電瓶嗎？

B：No problem, sir.
沒問題的，先生。

A：By the way, would you like to check the tires and clean the windshield?
對了，可以幫我檢查輪胎和清洗雨刷嗎？

永續圖書
線上購物網

www.foreverbooks.com.tw

◆ 加入會員即享活動及會員折扣。

◆ 每月均有優惠活動，期期不同。

◆ 新加入會員三天內訂購書籍不限本數金額，
即贈送精選書籍一本。（依網站標示為主）

專業圖書發行、書局經銷、圖書出版

永續圖書總代理：

五觀藝術出版社、培育文化、棋茵出版社、大拓文化、讀
品文化、雅典文化、知音人文化、手藝家出版社、璞申文
化、智學堂文化、語言鳥文化

活動期內，永續圖書將保留變更或終止該活動之權利及最終決定權。

旅遊英語萬用手冊

雅致風靡　典藏文化

親愛的顧客您好，感謝您購買這本書。

為了提供您更好的服務品質，煩請填寫下列回函資料，您的支持是我們最大的動力。

您可以選擇傳真、掃描或用本公司準備的免郵回函寄回，謝謝。

姓名：	性別：	□男　　□女
出生日期：　年　　月　　日	電話：	
學歷：	職業：	□男　　□女
E-mail：		
地址：□□□		
從何得知本書消息：□逛書店 □朋友推薦 □DM廣告 □網路雜誌		
購買本書動機：□封面 □書名□排版 □內容 □價格便宜		
你對本書的意見： 內容：□滿意□尚可□待改進　　編輯：□滿意□尚可□待改進 封面：□滿意□尚可□待改進　　定價：□滿意□尚可□待改進		
其他建議：		

總經銷：永續圖書有限公司

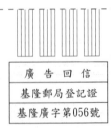

永續圖書線上購物網
www.foreverbooks.com.tw

您可以使用以下方式將回函寄回。

您的回覆，是我們進步的最大動力，謝謝。

① 使用本公司準備的免郵回函寄回。

② 傳真電話：（02）8647-3660

③ 掃描圖檔寄到電子信箱：

　 yungjiuh@ms45.hinet.net

沿此線對折後寄回，謝謝。

廣 告 回 信

基隆郵局登記證

基隆廣字第056號

2 2 1 0 3

 雅典文化事業有限公司　收
新北市汐止區大同路三段194號9樓之1

雅致風靡　典藏文化